THE MIGHTY ANCHOR

ROGUE ACADEMY, BOOK THREE

CARRIE AARONS

Copyright © 2019 by Carrie Aarons

All rights reserved.

No part of this book may be reproduced in any form or by any electronic or mechanical means, including information storage and retrieval systems, without written permission from the author, except for the use of brief quotations in a book review.

This is a work of fiction. Names, characters, businesses, places, events and incidents are either the products of the author's imagination or used in a fictitious manner. Any resemblance to actual persons, living or dead, or actual events is purely coincidental.

Editing done by Proofing Style.

Cover designed by Okay Creations.

Do you want your **FREE** Carrie Aarons eBook?

All you have to do is **sign up for my newsletter**, and you'll immediately receive your free book!

For the mightiest anchor I know - MBK.

PROLOGUE
VANCE

Christmas Day, Four Years Ago

Tourists don't understand how to walk on this beach.

With its rocky surface, deep undercurrent and rough around the edges charm, it intimidates them. The jagged fracture of the stones beneath their feet don't gel with the idea of a shoreline, at least not the ones we dream up in our imaginations when daydreaming about islands. They most certainly don't stroll along the difficult expanses barefoot.

No, the coastline of Brighton is reserved for its residents, and mainly, I've always thought, me.

A lot like this surly landscape, I compare myself to its rigidity, its unchanging and unrelenting nature. The water and sand of my hometown haunt are seldom noisy unless made to be that way by a sudden storm. The tide does not abandon the shore, the true instinct of it completely loyal to a fault. While some might look upon the scene before me and judge it for not being flashy or outright beautiful, I can see its true colors. Sometimes, the real allure of a thing comes from within its core.

On this beach, I am always certain of who I am, even if I can't grasp it often out there in the noisy world I've solidified myself into.

All the townspeople have long taken up in their comfy chairs, bellies full and merriment just beginning to fade from the Christmas Day festivities. Presents have been opened, family has been visited, and the duties of the holiday have been seen to.

In my house, my parents are quietly reading on the same couch in the study, my sister is upstairs applying her latest makeup gift. Me? I suffered through the day, rolling my eyes in secret at the ridiculous charade of greeting and small-talking with relations who only want to pry into my life for the publicity it may earn them.

Last year, I made the mistake of telling Aunt Henrietta, my mother's sister, that there was talk I'd be sold to an Italian league team. Lo and behold, what story do you think ended up in the papers on Boxing Day?

Now, I keep my mouth shut where the busybodies are concerned. Smile, nod, grit my teeth and bear it until they vacate the premises. The premises that my signing bonus bought.

Not that I hold ill will toward my own immediate family. No, Mum and Dad did a splendid job with what they had when Susie and I were growing up. It's nice to be able to come home, even for a day or two, to spend Christmas with them. The people I'm loyal to, I'm extremely loyal to. They can go a little wonky, cock something up, and I'll be there to clean up the mess. To those who show me devotion, I will give it back tenfold.

But ... I need my space. Something happens inside me with all of those people, chattering on around me for hours on end. My chest begins to shrink, my lungs fold in on themselves until I feel as if there's a vise squeezing my internal organs. Until I can't breathe. A sports doctor I saw long ago once told me I suffer from social anxiety, but the macho side of me wouldn't allow it to be true.

I've never sought help, I simply suffer through it until I can escape to the open, quiet, dark part of the world.

It's why my parents didn't question me when I stumbled out of the house in search of solitude. Blimey, they probably knew this was my hiding spot of choice.

I've been slowly walking along, my hands in my corduroy Christmas slacks, breathing in the frigid, peaceful night air, when I realize I'm not alone.

A few feet away, someone sits under the moonlight, a haunting song floating through the icy wind.

The quiet melody sweeps into my ears, pulling me closer as if it's a siren luring a sailor to its mesmerizing tune. Over the crash of the waves on the rock, I can barely make out the words.

"This year's love had better last .... heaven knows it's high time ..."

The David Gray song, a popular holiday song on the radio stations around Brighton and Clavering, where I spend the majority of the year, has always struck a somber chord in me. Most would say it's hopeful, that the singer was giving everlasting love just one more shot after being gutted so many times before.

The way I see it, it's a man trapped in an endless cycle of self-masochism. Who wants to open up his arms and fall into the sweet lies he knows are waiting?

I'm about to roll my eyes and walk off in the other direction, pitying the daft fool who'd take pointers from that song.

Until I glimpse a flutter of daisy gold hair, and I'm rooted to the spot.

It's her.

Hair that resembles the finest gold in a jeweler's case, with pale skin the color of creamy, almond milk. In the breeze, those infinite, straight locks swirl around her, the thin profile of her face catching a sliver of moonlight.

Lara Logan looks like something out of a hazy daydream, or maybe a nightmare ... the etherealness of her willing my feet to move.

She moved in across the street after I'd already left for the academy. The first time I saw her, I was ten and had come home for my dad's birthday. There she was, this blond little gangly thing, crouched in the dirt. Without thinking, I'd gone over and asked her what she was looking at. When she turned her eyes up to me, so blue it was like looking into the heart of the sea, I was a goner.

From the moment she pointed at the baby bunny nest she was observing, whispering that weren't they just so beautiful, I'd been completely smitten.

But my life was in Clavering. My soul was dedicated to football, and nothing else came close. So for eight years, I've watched her from afar. Pined as she turned into a woman, those gangly limbs transforming into slim curves and elegance. Dreamed about what she did, who she saw ... what a normal life for a normal girl must be like.

Not that there's anything *normal* about Lara in my eyes.

And now, here she is. Lara Logan, sitting on the same beach, on the same Christmas night. All alone, just like me.

In this moment, she turns her head up, as if she was expecting me. Her mouth opens slightly, the subtle pink of her lipstick smudging where she sinks her teeth into the right side of her bottom lip. Neither of us say anything as I sit down beside her, my shoes pointing toward the tide as I rest my elbows on my knees.

Our gazes connect, lingering, studying. We are strangers, but there is something under the surface ... a familiarity that begs to be poked at.

"Won't ya kiss me on that midnight street? Sweep me off my feet, singing, 'ain't this life so sweet?' ... This year's love had better last ..."

The lyrics bubble up between us from the speaker on her mobile, the screen of it turned down into the rocks so as to avoid any artificial light. I'm not sure what comes over me. Maybe it's the faux cheer infused in the air from the holiday. Maybe it's a right place, right time kind of scenario. Maybe it's because there is an urgent sense that if I don't do this, I will regret it for the rest of my bloody life.

Taking her jaw in my palm, I stroke a thumb over it, caressing her cold skin with the pad of my finger. Her eyes ignite, the white hot blue of her irises sparking. Lara doesn't pull away, but she doesn't lean in either. This is a creature wholly aware of her power, and what I need to do to harness it.

She's not the type of girl who wants to be asked to be kissed. I'm not sure how I know this, I just do. She also does not want to be tamed, or controlled. We're level, the two of us.

So I lean in, a fraction at a time, until our lips are lined up.

I sink my mouth onto hers at the exact moment a wave crashes to the rocks, drowning out all thought and the world around us.

Little did I know, that split-second decision would take my solid existence and change the course of it forever. Like a ship in the midst of a storm, everything I knew about myself, or held dear, was about to be thrown into the depths of the ocean.

And who I emerged as, who we emerged as, was something else entirely.

1

LARA

Watching as my son walks off, his little pudgy hand enveloped in his teacher's gentle grasp, I have to bite back a sob of complete and utter devastation.

It should be illegal to have to leave your child with someone else while you work for a living. Some days, when I'm caught up in the idealism of motherhood and how a utopian society should run I truly think this. The realistic, modern woman in me knows that not only is it not possible for ninety-nine percent of the population but that I truly love my job and wouldn't want to completely give it up.

But as I drop my beautiful boy off at nursery school, it's like carving out a piece of my heart and letting it walk around in the world by itself. I'm actively missing a chunk of my soul when I'm forced to set him down, to wave goodbye and then get in my car and drive away.

I know I'm creating a life for us, providing for him, showing him how strong a woman can be. I know I'm an ace role model for him, and I'm active and attentive when he's with me. But it doesn't make the sting of it hurt less.

"All right, bub, Mummy loves you!" I call out desperately, wanting him to turn around just one more time.

Like the brilliant boy he is, he obliges. Waving his fat little fingers, and giving me that mega-watt smile with his missing lower canine tooth, he yells excitedly, "Cheerio, Mummy!"

And then he disappears inside, off for a day of learning, friends, and fun.

My heart sinks, as it has been doing since the day I went back to work when he was only four months old. Having a baby without a partner at the age of twenty doesn't afford one much of a maternity leave. Not when you have things like rent, electric bills, car loans, and the other million things I have to worry about.

As if the universe and my self-loathing aren't trying to guilt me enough about being a shite mum this morning, I bump into the ultimate test as I descend the nursery school steps.

"Morning, Lara. Didn't realize you had to get Mason out the door so early. Isn't that such a pity?"

Turning, I have to bite down on my back molars hard to keep from reminding Portia that she too had to send her daughter to nursery school. We were in the same boat, both working mums. But apparently, since I became pregnant out of wedlock and still hadn't reached the age of twenty-three, that made me lesser. In her eyes, and the eyes of the other parents at Brighton Sea Nursery School, I was a chav.

Portia stands a head above me in her posh black heels as she ushers Reese, a two-year-old girl with bright red hair and gap teeth, along up the front steps of the building. She thinks she's intimidating, a businesswoman with a more important reason to leave her child in the care of another during the day.

"Well, I have to be in my classroom by seven thirty, so yes, it's up and at 'em in our flat." I put on a cheery smile, careful not to smooth the hem of my short-sleeved cotton dress.

She clucks her tongue, giving the mother behind her, one of her minions, a faux sympathetic look on my behalf.

"That is such a shame. You know, you might ask Miss Hayne about a teaching position here? That way you could actively participate in raising your son, and wouldn't have to leave him for such a silly reason. She might even allow you partial tuition!"

As if my job as a secondary school English teacher was a pathetic excuse for enrolling Mason in nursery school. And as if my salary wasn't competitive, I didn't receive health benefits and wasn't saving toward a better future for both my son and me.

As if I hadn't struck out on my own, refusing the help of my mother and father, when I found out I was having a little boy. I'd carved a life for Mason and myself, through sweat, blood, and tears I'd struggled through the toughest of times for myself and my child.

It was a bloody sad thing that words from a miserable cow could render all of that meager.

Trying to expel a steady breath, I'm about to supply some cheeky comeback, when my mobile buzzes.

Pulling it out, the feeling of dread I've been trying to swallow for the past few weeks manifests itself like a cold fist in the middle of my chest.

Vance: *I'm in town. I want to see Mason. And we need to talk.*

He's been warning me for weeks, via text message, that he's coming back to Brighton.

The place where he grew up. The place where I grew up. The place where *our* son was born.

I have bigger fish to worry about than Portia and her belittling comments. I walk off, completely leaving her in the middle of the dressing down she was issuing. I'm sure I'll be called some kind of awful name for that, but it'll be behind my back, so I don't really care.

If anyone finds out who my son's father really is, there would be much more scrutiny than the typical nursery school gossip.

As it is, I'm in a panic that my son's father found out he is a father. Vance Morley left me high and dry ... well, I guess not dry. He left me pregnant ... not that he knew that. I'm explaining this terribly.

It goes like this. I'd been smitten from the moment I laid eyes on Vance, the boy who lived across the street, when I was ten. At eighteen, he'd come home from his football academy, found me on the beach at Christmas, and snogged the daylights out of me. What began after that was a tumultuous, passionate, mental long-distance affair. We fought hard; we loved harder. I called things off, and he came begging back. He called things off, and I came begging back.

In the end, though, the root of our problem was that I wasn't the highest priority in his life. And for a girl who grew up knowing exactly what her worth should be in a relationship, I couldn't handle that.

Football is his wife. I was his mistress. And there was no way I was settling for anything less than exceptional love.

But Vance Morley had left one parting gift ... the little boy I just let walk away with a chunk of my heart. The reason his father is on my case about seeing him, and about talking?

I *may* have been bitter about our final break up. Vance had cut things off ruthlessly, and I took it upon myself to keep the secret of his child from him ... for more than two years. The way he left me, he didn't deserve the love and light that sweet boy brought into the world.

My temples throb as I slam the driver door of my creaky old Saab shut, the frigid autumn wind invading the inside of the door and rattling my bones. It's barely past dawn and already I have a headache. Twisting the diamond on my ring finger, I feel marginally better. Now, if only I had time for a stop at the coffee shop before my first period class.

I'm an independent woman; a caustic, socially paranoid person who hasn't had the easiest road to walk in my life. When I found out that Mason was growing in my belly, I gave myself one day. One day to mentally break down, to worry about feeding, clothing, and taking care of a child while not losing myself or my dreams in the process. To mourn the loss of my childhood, of the twenties I'd only just started.

And then, I dusted myself off. I went to night school, after waitressing during the day, to earn my teaching license. I applied for jobs, rented my first flat, read every baby book I could get my hands on and made it work.

I'd done it all without Vance Morley. Without his pigheaded stubbornness, or his arrogant, quiet charm. Without his intense looks that could paralyze me from halfway across a room. Without his foul mouth or protective embrace.

The man walked out of my life, and now that he saw what he'd given up, he wanted back in.

Well, I have news for him. And I know for a fact, from extensive experience dealing with the brute, that he isn't going to like it.

He isn't going to like it at all.

2

VANCE

The first time I saw my son, I just about fainted.

Mum had asked me to run down to a shop she liked near the beach, for a bottle of wine to serve with dinner. Dad's business partner was coming, and she was serving shepherd's pie. I wasn't home much and thought I could at least complete the simple task of buying the night's alcohol. By all accounts, Dad's partner was a dry bloke and I thought I'd need the aid of a good buzz.

Things at the Rogue Soccer Academy, the football organization I'd been signed to when I was eight years old, had been going well. I lived on the campus in Clavering, about a two-hour drive from Brighton, for almost ten years. While I love my family, I'd adopted two brothers-in-arms while at the academy, Jude Davies and Kingston Phillips. Together, they called us the three horsemen of the football apocalypse ... someday soon we'd bring honor and many World Cup trophies to England.

But, four years later, I'm still stuck at the academy, riding the proverbial bench, while Jude and Kingston start for Rogue Football Club in London. I'm stuck in limbo, both professionally, and as I discovered mere weeks ago, personally.

It was midday when I'd walked out of the shop, a bag containing four bottles of wine in my hand, when I caught Lara in my peripheral. I hadn't seen her since we broke things off more than two years ago.

She looked ... magnificent. She'd cut her golden locks into that trendy style all the girls were wearing these days. Just above her shoulders, with a longer angle in the front and some fringe swept to the side. It still curled around the edges of her face, her high cheekbones dusted with color and eyelashes that were inky black and kissed her cheeks each time she blinked. The long tan trench coat over olive-green slacks and a cream-colored sweater made her look impossibly chic.

The whole ensemble made Lara appear much more mature than the teenage girl in a crop top and faded denim shorts who dared me to skinny dip in the ocean after a rave one night. But, her change in appearance hadn't deterred my heart from slamming into my rib cage, threatening to dislodge itself from my body in an attempt to make its way back to her.

And then ... I saw him. He came bounding out of the shop she'd been in, carrying a lollipop that was almost the size of his head. The little boy, the one who ran up to her shrieking "Mummy!"

He had my hair. And her eyes. And a slope of a nose that exactly matched my father's. His chin was all Lara, but then I saw the boy smile, and bloody hell ...
The same dimple I have in my left cheek appeared.

The bag dropped from my hand, two of the wine bottles shattering right there on the sidewalk. Lara and the boy startled, whipping their heads my way.

I heard her audible gasp from across the busy Brighton street. Up until that moment, she hadn't spotted me. I'd had a few minutes to collect myself, to watch her from afar and observe the person who, at one time, had known me more intimately than anyone.

If I had a nostalgic grin, a bittersweet thump of my heart, or an idea to walk up to her and see how she'd been doing ... that kindness flew out the bloody window.

The minute I'd seen my son.

It was clear that Lara believed she was staring at a literal ghost as she gaped at me. Bending at the waist, without taking her eyes off mine, she grabbed her son, pulling him up into her arms and smooshing his cheek against hers. The toddler, with his chubbiest cheeks, giggled as if his mother is playing a silly game.

And I was across the road, running into traffic without a care for bodily harm, in two seconds flat.

"Something you want to tell me?" Never one for small talk or pleasantries, I tower over the woman who'd bewitched my heart since the moment I kissed her on our hometown beach one Christmas.

Lara's mouth falls open, gaping and floundering like a fish struggling for breath on the bottom of a boat. "Vance ... I ... what are you doing here?"

"I'll be the one asking the bloody questions." I could hardly believe my eyes as I stared down at the little boy in her arms, the one trying to fit the entire stick of candy he was holding in his mouth.

"Watch your language." *Her voice is harsh, those rich blue eyes cutting me down as they flit from me to the toddler.*

"Lara, is he mine?" *I almost choke on the words.*

People are starting to stare, and I know that it's because of who I am. I can't return to Brighton without being stopped on the streets, without being asked for an autograph or a handout. I'm not Jude Davies, but I do all right. My own car, buying my parents their house. I have money in the bank, loads of it saved for the day when my body can no longer play the sport I love with every part of my soul. Heaven knows I don't squander my wealth on flashy purchases like Kingston Phillips. No, I am steady, dependable, middle of the road one, both with my finances, and in life.

And steady, dependable, solid as a boulder Vance Morley didn't get birds pregnant and not know about children he fathered. I'm just as furious at myself as I am with Lara at this moment.

Lara must realize that we're drawing attention, because she grabs my arm, pulling me around the block and into an alleyway. The boy on her hip coos, giggling as he bounces at the hurried pace she's keeping. My wine is somewhere on the street, forgotten. Everything but right now is forgotten.

Once we're out of the earshot of bystanders, she whips around, cradling her son to her as if I might steal him. My vision snags on the ring she's wearing on her left hand. A small, round diamond set on a gold band.

She's engaged? The thought throttles through my brain, shooting down my spine and into my heart like a shock of electricity. Lara, my Lara, is with someone else? I don't even have time to address the agony ripping the organ in my chest to shreds, because her voice cuts through the pain.

"What do you think, Vance? Look at him, you're not daft!" Her tone is meant to be offensive, as if I'm the one who did something wrong here.

"Why are you acting like I'm the one who's committed a crime here? I asked a question to a fact that I was, apparently, never aware of! Or were you just going to keep this secret from me and from him for the rest of our lives?"

I want to punch something. The brick next to Lara's head looks mighty tempting. But I hold off, knowing that if I unleash the beast threatening to explode from my chest, I won't be able to cram him back in.

"His name is Mason," she says quietly.

I'd been so stunned into silence after she told me his name, that I couldn't talk. It provided Lara with an escape, and she scooted out from under my glower. And since that day, just five or so weeks ago, I haven't seen my son. Each text I've sent, all the calls I've made to Lara ... they've gone unanswered. I know I might not have handled the initial meeting or my confronting her as well as I could have ... but bloody hell, she hid my son from me.

Mason. I have a son and his name is Mason. That fact has blown my world to smithereens, it obliterated my ability to speak for hours. I stood in that alley long after Lara retreated with our child. I pictured his face and felt my entire world shift on its axis. Nothing means what it used to, and somehow my five senses feel different. My skin feels too tight, and I can't figure out which way is up.

I'm a father. And how much of his life have I already missed?

The compulsive part of me, the perfectionist that lives in my gut, is fraught with grief and failure. My son doesn't know me. I've missed so many major moments in his life, and I'll never get those back.

That's why I am back in Brighton. I gave Headmaster Darnot, the prick who runs the Rogue Academy, an official notice of leave this morning. It only affords me two weeks to tend to my business, and then I have to be back on the pitch for the second squad. Football is my passion, the reason I wake up in the morning and why I was put on this earth. I truly believe that. But, in the more recent past, the club I work so hard for didn't believe in me.

As a twenty-two-year-old keeper, who gives every ounce of sweat and blood I have to the sport, I should be playing at a top-level club on an international scale. But because RFC has a brilliant keeper, Remus Bayern, who is in his prime and winning matches for them left and right, I'm relegated to the academy until they're ready to call me up. But who knows when that will be ... it could be never. They're keeping me in Clavering, among the lads just learning how to play, in my best years. They can't even show me mercy enough to let me go, or sell me to another club so that I can play my greatest years on a first squad.

I'm as loyal as they come, but once I learned about Mason, I knew it was time to be selfish. When it came to Rogue, *and* when it came to Lara. I've sat idly by for too long, both on the football bench and when it came to sorting things with my ex.

As I drive along the coastal road, my vision skates over the stone beach where I first kissed her.

I'm back in town, and I'm not leaving without the two people I came here for.

3
LARA

We're only two months into the school year, and already I can feel my students tuning me out as I begin to flip open my copy of *David Copperfield*.

"There is this idea that Dickens evokes in this novel, that of being our own hero or allowing someone else to be the hero of our life. How do you think you can be the hero of your own story?"

I ask the question and get crickets. Pure silence, the kind that makes educators cringe with self-doubt. I swear, I do love my profession, but when I decided to throw caution to the wind and get my teaching license when I was pregnant at the age of twenty ... I thought I'd be inspiring a bit more than I do now.

Granted, it is the last hour of the school day, and these students have probably been through a full teenage life cycle before they make it to my English class. A girl in the front row has red-rimmed eyes, indicating a fight with her best mate or the boyfriend she's probably been seeing for all of a week's time. Someone in here smells like an ashtray, and I can tell that person has been sneaking an electric cigarette in the bathroom. Two blokes near the back are poorly hiding the fact that they're using their mobiles under the desk, and a young lady in the middle row, seated next to my other whiteboard, is scarfing down lunch. I wonder, idly, what caused her to miss her lunch hour that she's only now eating her peanut butter sandwich.

A timid hand catches my attention, and I latch onto it.

"Yes!" I point my finger at Tommy, a black-haired boy with blue-rimmed glasses, who is one of the only souls in here to indulge my discussions.

I'm not normally so naff, on the contrary, I know for a fact I'm considered one of the ace teachers at Brighton Secondary School. But this group of students has proven to be particularly difficult to engage, so I'm putting in all the pep I've got.

"Well ... I think that David doesn't end up being the hero of his own story. He's an observer, not an active participant in his own life. And while that might allow him to be a better writer he's only witnessing the moments. He's letting them pass him by. What I took from the book is that we have to be do-ers, if we want to be our own hero."

My heart sings, because if I've only gotten through to one person today, if the literary works I love so much have spoken to a student as much as they speak to me ... then that answer hit the nail brilliantly on the head.

"Well done, Tommy. Through David's inaction, I've always thought Dickens was trying to tell his reader that we must not be merely witnesses to what happens around us."

"But in order to act, to be our own hero, one needs the qualities in his or her personality to do that," Kitson, the girl who was just munching her sandwich, speaks up.

Her eyes dart around, and I know she needs a push, so I give her one. "Interesting point, how do you mean?"

She shrugs her shoulders, her eyes shooting down to the desk. "David is naïve in his childish trust of other people. He doesn't read social cues well, allows others to take advantage of him. If you don't understand the vicious world you're walking into, I can believe that it's hard to be the hero of your story."

Bugger all, what happened to this girl today?

Nodding my head slowly, I try to spin her depressing views into a positive. It might be the hardest task as a teacher, taking the bad things and making them good. Novels like to do this for us, sometimes, but there are always the students who will interpret it into melancholy. Teaching is not unlike parenting in that way, and it makes me anxious for the years ahead with Mason.

"That's not untrue ... but perhaps having those qualities initially can create a balance that makes a better, more compassionate hero? If you trust, and are burned, maybe you learn from that. And then through that lesson, you can become your own hero. Take those child-like, wonderful qualities and merge them with the hardened experience of someone who has been through tough times. I think, then, you can be your hero."

I know I did, I want to add. But this isn't the time for a confession of my deepest character flaws. My eyes linger on Kitson's, and I know she's internally chewing over the brain food I just gave her.

If she's anything like me, she'll take that idea and use it to construct the life she wants for herself. Because as melancholy as the thought is, no one is coming to save her.

A few minutes later, the final bell tolls, signaling the end of the day.

"Don't forget, your assignments on Dickens' life work are due on Monday!" I yell out the door at my retreating students' backs.

Hand to God, at least three of them will forget about the paper over the weekend and come in next week, pedaling excuses. I can't worry about that now, though. It's Friday, I'm done with work, and headed to see my son.

My mobile buzzes in the pocket of my coat as I walk out into the blustery parking lot of the school.

"Hi, love." I pick it up, a smile on my face.

"Someone is having a splendid time with his after school blueberry muffin snack." Louis's voice comes through the other end, and I can hear Mason in the background, babbling on.

"Has he smashed it into his clothes and hair?" I chuckle, picturing my chubby-cheeked toddler cackling while caking food on every part of himself.

Louis chuckles with me. "Oh, yes. We'll have to throw him in the rubbish bin!"

I hear Mason clapping and giggling, because he thinks the word rubbish is hilarious. The sheer amount that he knows and picks up on now astounds me daily, most days I can't believe he grew in my belly and at one time just laid on my chest for hours on end.

I also can't believe I have a fiancé who watches my son when I can't pick him up early from nursery school on Friday. After Vance, I never thought I'd find love again. That sounds cliché and daft, but it's true. What we had was intense, all-consuming—that first time kind of love that you remember forever and compare everything that comes after it to.

Louis walked into my life when I was four months pregnant, fresh off a heart-wrenching breakup, and so bogged down in preparing for the life I wanted, that I barely gave him the time of day. No, really, I walked off when he asked me what time it was. We were standing at a bus stop, waiting for an eight a.m. bus that was going to take me to my course at the local university. Louis, with his kind brown eyes and average appearance, had turned to me and asked if I had the time, because he suspected the bus was late. I pretended not to hear him until he tapped me on the shoulder again and smiled down on me.

He was only meant to be a rebound. When he asked me for

dinner the next week, at that same bus stop, I'd thought, why not? I was hungry and short on money, and he seemed nice enough. He was a small-town prosecutor who'd grown up in Brighton and had been four years ahead of me in school.

What it turned into was a two-year relationship that resulted in an engagement. Louis had been next to me in the hospital when Mason was born; the revelation of my pregnancy never swayed his loyalty to our relationship. He's the man who helped me care for a colicky infant, and the responsible one who planned out my life insurance policy and will, God forbid something happens to me. Louis is the one who fixed my broken toilet and held me when I cried in those first months of us dating, even if we both quietly knew it was over Vance.

And on Mason's first birthday, he got down on one knee and presented me with a ring. There was no other answer I could give besides yes. Louis is a good man, and an excellent stand-in father. He cares for Mason like his own, and he is reliable, dependable.

Even if I don't love him with the passion of a thousand blazing suns ... I can be happy in a life with him.

"Listen, we have that meeting with the caterer tomorrow. You've still got your mum coming to watch Mason, right?"

A thud of guilt drops onto my heart like a boulder. Not only have I completely forgotten about the wedding appointment we have tomorrow, but the age-old shame of my baby's father kicks at the rusted organ like a car that won't start properly.

To this day, Louis and I have never discussed who fathered Mason. He tried to broach the subject only twice, both of which I shut down quicker than a laptop from the nineties. Now, he doesn't bring it up, and I don't supply anything.

My mobile burns in my hand, and part of my brain thinks it's trying to kill me, with the text from Vance still sitting in my messages, unanswered.

He's back in town, and now I'm going to have to face the music. Maybe there is a way I can pander to him, convince him to forget about what he saw and leave my satisfactory life intact.

The logical part of me knows there is a hell-storm coming, and I'm going to perish or survive.

"Yes, she's coming. I have to run out before the meeting, but I'll be there," I tell him, not alluding to the reason for my upcoming early Saturday morning disappearance.

In truth, missing the meeting with the caterer sparks a flame of hope in my chest. If I'm not there, I don't have to hear about the wedding. If I'm not there, I don't have to make active decisions about marrying a man who, as awful as it sounds, is my second choice.

I wonder what Charles Dickens commentary would be on those actions? On taking a back seat and witnessing my own life ...

Instead, after I ring off with Louis, I open up my messages and begin to type.

Lara: *Fine. I'll meet you tomorrow morning. The café by your parent's new house, 9 a.m.*

Pandora's box has been opened, and my heart thumps at the knowledge that I probably won't be able to snap the lid on tight again.

4

VANCE

A blaze of struggling breath, incinerated muscle, and waning adrenaline push me through the last of my sprint; the end of the pitch coming into view as my feet carry me closer and closer.

Once I reach it, the far end of the grass crying out to me like a welcome mattress, I collapse onto my knees, sucking in lungfuls of air as if I'm about to slip under the ocean.

The soreness sets in, a rage of wildfire licking up my legs and into my back, down my shoulders and even out into my fingers until I'm flexing them to get the cramps out.

Just because I'm not at the academy doesn't mean I don't need to train. There is a match I'm expected back for in just a week and a half, and if I'm not in top form, I'll risk the clean sheet I've been working for. I already have three this season, not that it means as much when I'm playing for the secondary squad at the academy. But I've never been a slacker or one to rely on talent alone.

Which is why I am up at the crack of dawn, punishing my body through an intense conditioning session in hopes that it will not only strengthen my body, but my mind.

In just an hour's time, I'm having a sit down with Lara. My hands shake with the knowledge, and to my very core, I'm rattled. I'm not an easily affected person ... I pride myself on the steady, fair approach I take to life.

But when it comes to Lara Logan, I'm never bloody prepared. The woman throws me off my game, every time. It's why I left. It's why I've thought about her every goddamn minute since I walked away.

Somewhere within the bowels of the stadium, a sound echoes, making me look up.

I know a few of the blokes who suit up for the premier league squad in Brighton, simply through the channels that most athletes know each other ... or I played with them or against them in their academy days. So it's with their blessing that I'm allowed access to the facilities for the two weeks I'm in Brighton on leave. None of them know, or bothered to ask, why I'm here, but I'm grateful that I get to keep up my regimen in peace while using state-of-the-art equipment. The Brighton by the Sea Football Club is in the premier league, but not typically referred to as being among the elite, like Rogue and the others that reside in London. It's looked upon as second tier, though it competes annually with the more posh clubs.

When I walked in two hours ago, I was the only soul around, but now there is someone walking across the pitch to me as I catch my breath. Standing, trying to appear as if I didn't almost just honk my protein shake onto the pitch.

"Vance, right?" A vaguely familiar-looking bloke sticks out his hand, a Brighton kit slung over his bare shoulders, matching shorts on his hips, and boots strapped on.

"That's right." I nod, shaking his hand.

"I'm Theo Binket."

Ah, their keeper. This bloke has the job I want, only at a different club. I've heard of Theo, he's mentioned in the same sentences as some of the up-and-coming goalies on the English football scene. Nowhere near as brilliant as Remus, or me I'd argue, but he's good in the net and seems like a decent bloke in his interviews.

"Nice to meet you. I'll get out of your hair, was just doing some training." A quick wave of my hand, and I'm off.

I'm not one for overstaying welcomes, conversing with strangers, or any other general niceties. That's Kingston's task in our trio, the charmer. The one who diverts attention from both Jude and I so that we don't have to extend ourselves. He takes pleasure in it, not sure why. And when he's not around, the honor falls to Jude. I'm the last resort when it comes to brokering a conversation, and when I'm forced to, I typically opt not to do it anyway.

"Before the sun rose, eh? Yeah, I've heard you're a machine."

I turn, giving him a nod that, indeed, I am a machine. While I might be introverted, I'm not one to shy away from my strengths. I'm dedicated and relentless; I'm not humble enough to forego boasting about it, even if it's done without words. After all, I'm still a professional athlete; the job requires a healthy dose of ego.

"Hard work doesn't work unless you do." I quote one of my favorite sayings.

"Ain't that the truth. It's a lonely world as a keeper, it's why I'm here most mornings before all them lazy blokes arrive. You in town for long?"

Shaking my head, I don't let my expression convey a thing. "Not long."

Theo's lips turn up in a smile. "What they say about you is true, Vance. Well, if you want to grab a pint, you know where to find me. Keeper to keeper, it'd be nice to pick your brain."

His words don't even hit me, the armor I've placed over my heart just deflecting them with ease. Growing up in this world, you learn to develop a tough skin. I have a few close allies, and everyone else is against me. It's not paranoia, it's true. If I were gunning for Theo's job, which I could, we would be enemies. It's all the point of view of things.

Showering quickly and slipping into the jeans and sweater I brought, I shrug on my coat as I head for my car. Brighton is downright chilly, even for October. The ocean kicks up the frigid wind, sending it rolling through the streets and around the buildings. Though my skin is thick, it's not the hide against the weather I developed in my first eight years here. When you're an ocean town kind of child, you have a special immunity against the harsh winters here. Apparently, I lost that badge of honor.

The café Lara chose as our meeting spot is just a block from my parent's home, so I park my car at the house and walk over partly to prove to myself that I could hold up against the cold. But by the time I arrive, the warmth and aroma of baked goods seeping into my bones, my teeth are chattering. The place isn't one I figure Lara frequents often, which is why she asked me to meet her here. It caters to the wealthy part of Brighton, a small community of people who don't dare leave their beachfront solitude for the downtown area or the more average income parts of town.

When I'd seen her for the first time, all those years ago, it was on the lawns of our respective childhood homes, right across the street from one another. Back then, our financial situation hadn't been all that different. I was still a young player in the academy, sending nominal amounts of money home to my family so that it justified the club in stealing my childhood.

At least, looking back, that's what I consider it now. It was almost hush money, the system of taking young boys out of their home to raise them to be football machines. But, my parents stepped right on board. Not that I hold any grudge, it just is what it is. I wanted to play football; they knew that. It's the price we all paid.

But aside from the academy money, my parents made a decent living at average jobs. Lara was the product of a divorced household, living with her mum in the smallest bungalow-style home on the street. Her dad was around and helped to support them as I later found out. But we were both kids from middle-income families, growing up in an idyllic seaside town.

Once I signed my amateur contract, however, all of that changed. I took my family from not being able to afford a holiday every year to vacationing in a private villa in Italy. I bought my parent's an oceanfront home made of glass and steel, moved them away from the life they knew, and didn't stick around to see the changes.

It had been a point of contention when Lara and I had been together, the difference in our lifestyles.

Heading for the counter, I order myself a double espresso, needing the caffeine, and a black breakfast tea for Lara. It's her favorite, and I throw in a raspberry muffin knowing that might set her mood on a good track, as well.

I had plans for this conversation. It didn't surprise me that she wasn't pleased about my return to Brighton.

Just a minute after I take a seat at a table in the corner, the bell over the door jingles. And then there she is.

My lungs completely deflate, as they usually do in my initial time of seeing her at any given meeting. Lara is simply stunning.

Her sun-kissed hair is still skimming her shoulders, that sexy, modern cut making her appear, somehow, even more feminine and cutthroat at the same time. Her cheeks and nose are red from the wind, and I have the urge to walk to her and blow warm air on her hands, helping her adjust from the cold. That face, the one composed of sharp angles and creamy skin, has always captivated me. I think it's her eyes, how large and doll-like they are in a face that would otherwise be harsh. Big, blue as rare sapphires, and framed with thick black lashes, she aims her eyes right at me.

Butterflies, nasty, big bugs claw at the inside of my gut as she strolls to the table, a cream-colored sweater dress hugging her brilliantly as those brown boots make the toned legs eating up the distance between us look impossibly long.

"Vance." She says my name, not hello or some other variation of it.

So, that's how it's going to be. I swallow my ire, knowing that I'm not here for any other reason than to get my family back. I love this woman, when she isn't acting like the spawn of the devil, and I want to know my son. To get those things, I have to put every practiced behavior when it comes to Lara behind me.

"Thanks for meeting me," I say, my hands folded on the table as she sits.

I know that Lara is spiteful. The way I ended things, so cold and sterile as if our relationship was some business agreement that had run its course, was despicable. She deserved more than that. Hell, I did, too ... but I couldn't war within myself anymore. I'd gone mental, trying to choose between my love and desire for her, and the passion I have for football, that I couldn't bear it any longer. So I'd chosen the thing that had been the most constant in my life. The thing that didn't hurt so bad or make me question every facet of my life.

"You didn't give me much of a choice." She huffs.

"You didn't tell me I had a child, so let's not start accusations here," I shoot back, my anger bearing down like a gorilla sitting on my shoulders.

Lara is both the girl next door and the elusive cheeky bird; she's a good girl with her sights set on the straight and narrow. But there is this underlying mystery, as if she'll surprise you at any moment and veer of course just because she can. It's what drew me to her, and what makes her so difficult to understand. She cares deeply about other people, but can also go weeks without needing the interaction of another person.

At least that's how she was when I knew her.

"I don't even know where to start. How could you do this? When was he born? What is his birth date? Is he ... is he okay? Are you okay? Do you need anything? What does your mother say about this? How is she keeping this secret from my parents? I mean, I know they don't live across the street from each other anymore, but they're close, Lara."

She chews on her bottom lip, a behavior I know means she's extremely nervous. Tapping her fingers is when she was anxious, she shuffles on her feet when she's lying, lip chewing is for extreme nerves. When something is so funny that she belly-laughs, it's a silent noise, almost as if the hilarity is more than her body can produce a sound for. And when I put my lips on a certain place behind her ear, the raspy moan that emanated from her throat ...

Christ. I know all of her little tics. I know all of *her*.

"Well, it's not a secret she has to keep." She rubs the back of her neck, not daring to meet my eyes.

In the center of my chest, something wriggles free, and suddenly I understand what she's saying. This is worse than I thought it was.

"They don't know who his father is?" I snarl, the rage reaching a breaking point in my chest.

5
LARA

Vance looks like he might flip the table between us and begin trashing the entire café.

"Tell me, Lara. Tell me that you've hidden the fact that I'm his father from—bloody hell, everyone!"

Bloody hell, why does he still have this effect over me? Even sitting across this table from him, with all the guilt, hurt, and loathing floating around in my heart, I wish I could crawl into his lap, take his beard in my hands, and kiss him until we've both lost all thought.

The man is a giant, one of those people who not only have an enormous frame but the way he holds it makes him imposing. Vance always suck the air out of a room; all eyes go to him when he walks through the door. With his six-foot-five body towering over everyone else, the intense eyes that are so dark they look almost black, and jet-black hair and beard it's impossible to notice anything else when he's in your presence. Not to mention the mass of muscles that he's carved into every portion of his body, the man is formidable.

To most, he looks like the kind of man who could take down

a bear. But when you really get to the heart of Vance Morley, he's a gentle, observant, wise, mild-mannered person.

And one who still makes my insides quiver with the heat of a wildfire, licking up my spine in uncontrollable gusts. The chocolate-eyed bastard always had this overwhelming effect on me, as if my heart turns to putty when he steps a hundred yards in my vicinity.

Squaring my shoulders, I prepare for a row. "I hid that fact. No one knows you're his father."

My eyes flicker to his chest, because I swear I can hear his heart audibly break. I can hear my own splinter, too. This isn't easy for me, beyond any means. I hate that I put that wounded expression on his face, and I loathe even more that Mason doesn't know his father.

It might seem like I'm an arse. That my harshness, my mean streak, is strictly dramatic and uncalled for. As I'm biased toward myself, I'll disagree, but in the timeline of everything that happened between us, it's an evident truth that I'm not overreacting to Vance's sudden one-eighty turnaround. And so, I have to stick up for myself. Ever since I started caring for a baby when no one thought I could do it alone, much less at all, I've been my only ally.

"You wanted nothing to do with me two years ago. Said I was a weight that you couldn't carry anymore, those were your exact words, Vance. You're the one who ruined us, who threw everything we had away like it didn't matter at all. What was I supposed to do when I found out I was pregnant? Tell the man who'd just told me I didn't fit into his plan that he had a child on the way? Can't you understand why I was hesitant to do that? You didn't want me, you made that crystal clear. What makes you think you would have wanted anything to do with our son?"

"Because he's my child!" Vance nearly roars and then seems to check himself. "I-I shouldn't have said those things. About you, about us. I was ... I didn't know how to handle it all. But that doesn't mean I wouldn't want Mason."

Something that's always sat like a lump in the back of my throat finally voices itself. "You wouldn't have told me to get rid of him? To end the pregnancy?"

There are plenty of things I feel guilty about, plenty of things I wish I could have talked over with Vance. But this was the one that stuck in my mind. The scenario that, even now, I couldn't help but obsess over. If I had told him all those years ago, would he have asked me to abort the baby?

It seems like everything in the café stills, like the windows go icy and all the warmth is taken out of the room—like the dementors from Harry Potter have arrived.

"You don't get to make hellacious assumptions on my character when you never even gave me the option of knowing."

The way he says the words, it's as if they're curses.

My heart withers, everything in me rolling from the tension of all of this. I attempt to gulp down the knot that's formed in my throat, but it doesn't work.

When I speak, it's with a croak. "What do you want, Vance?"

His eyes smolder, and a crackle of electricity lights my body with a bolt. Vance blinks down, focusing on the table for a moment, and then back up, never breaking his gaze from mine.

"There are a lot of things I want. I want to be the starting keeper for Rogue Football Club. I want to be different from how I inherently am. I want to stop being so bloody angry. I want to know my son. I want to hear his laugh and ask him everything he knows. I want to teach him to kick a ball. But what I want most of all, what I wish for more than anything, is to rip that fucking ring off your finger and put mine on it."

I'm not even sure he blinks when he completely destroys the world as I know it.

Maybe I'm the sinner, and he's the saint. Maybe it's the other way around.

Either way, there are plenty of fingers to point.

When it all comes down to it, though my heart still wants to walk out of this café with him. It wants to surrender itself, no matter if he sticks a knife through it.

And now, I'm even more terrified than I was before I came here. If I thought I could just keep moving, keep my feet on the right path and not dare look back, I could pretend that our chapter was over.

That couldn't be more of a lie.

6

VANCE

Lara thought I was being hasty, that the words I told her couldn't be trusted.

It must seem strange to her, my desire to be a family. To invite everything I told her I didn't want into my life.

But the moment I'd seen her holding Mason, his cheek pressed to hers, everything clicked into place. Before, my world was off-kilter, but I'd glimpsed the woman I love cradling our child, and the universe righted itself.

I want to kick myself in the bollocks for being so daft two years ago. Lara and I constantly fought—fights that stemmed from my commitment issues. I was a dog, a foul git who didn't give her the care and attention she deserved.

Here she was, a woman whose parents had divorced in her childhood, and I had unwittingly placed the same predicament on her life. She was wrong for not telling me. *Christ*, how my veins burned with the fury I felt for missing the first years of my son's life. But I know that she would never have chosen this if she thought I'd stick around for her.

For our entire relationship, I had one foot out the door. I can't imagine the mental state she had to be in finding out she was pregnant so young, and thinking that the father of her child had chosen a bigger and better path than her.

Bloody hell, I want to kick myself in the bollocks for how I treated her.

"And what did she say?" Jude asks in my ear, my mobile pressed against my shoulder.

I've just filled him in on what I confessed to Lara. How I want her back, how I want us to be a family.

"She was so shocked, I thought she might just throw her tea in my face. Before she could collect herself, I asked if I could see Mason. Well, pretty much bloody demanded it. It's bad enough she hid the pregnancy from me, but I could take serious legal action now if she doesn't let me near him."

"You wouldn't do that, mate," Jude scolds me.

"Of course, I wouldn't, but she doesn't know that. If I can use it as leverage, I can put my plan to work."

"I've never heard you so … devious. I'm afraid I might prefer this Vance better, with his masterful mission. What's the plan?"

I shrug as if my best mate can see me. "Honestly, I don't have one. But I know I'm not playing mister nice guy anymore. It's gotten me nowhere, both personally and professionally. The time is up on courteousness."

Transferring the pot of water to the stove burner, I click it on and watch as the steel cloud with steam from the fire below. When I come home, I like to cook for my family. It's something I do well, since having taught myself while living at Rogue Academy. Sure, there is a full-service dining hall, but someone had to cook for Kingston and Jude on the late nights where too much alcohol was involved. And, there is a satisfaction I get from cooking and serving an entire meal; the steps involved, the mindless prep work, the completion and presentation that impresses even the smallest group of people. Cooking is something that takes my thoughts away from all the stress in my life.

Plus, my parents never ask much of me and have stayed out of my business when I showed up unexpectedly on their doorstep and told them I was on leave. I've done a lot for my family since signing my amateur contract, but I still feel I owe them more. My parents are supportive, understanding, gracious. My sister appreciates all I've done for her, such as sending her to uni and paying for a lot of the things my parents couldn't afford. They've all done so without expectation that I should help them financially and have instead focused on building me up and helping me follow my dream.

As far as families go, I know how lucky I am. I'm not one to forget that, or not show my appreciation.

And eventually, I am going to have to tell them about the baby. About the son I have that they don't know. How Lara had hidden the truth from me. They have to know she has a child, and it is not going to go down well when they discover that I'm the father and that she's kept their grandchild from them.

But tonight, it's just about a nice family meal and showing them my love through actions, such as cooking, and not words. I've never been particularly verbal with my affection, a fact that got me into trouble with Lara plenty of times.

"Do you mean ... are you considering leaving Rogue?" Jude asks, his tone puzzled.

Of course, my football-obsessed mate would pick up on that. So, I give him the truth. "I'm not sure ... I have only given it preliminary thoughts."

I don't continue, and I hear Jude's annoyed huff as I begin to dice tomatoes on the chopping board.

"All right, if we're doing away with the mister nice guy business, we also have to do away with the caveman silence. How about you just tell me what you're thinking, instead of making me drag it out of you? I've already been to Clavering once, don't think Aria and I won't come to Brighton to beat your feelings out of you."

That has a wry smile gracing my lips. "Fine, you don't have to be an arse. It's just that ... I've given my life to Rogue. And I'm at the point where I need it to pay off. And Niles, or Darnot, or whoever it is that determines my future, they haven't actually given me much of one. I'm wasting my paramount years of talent competing against bloody children, and I'm wound up."

Niles Harrington and Headmaster Darnot, two of the top decision makers in both the Rogue Football Academy and Rogue Football Club, have been withholding information about my future on the pitch for as long as I can remember.

"But it's always been the three of us," Jude argues, sounding hurt.

As the water begins to boil, I throw in the homemade spaghetti I made this morning. "Come on, mate. It hasn't. You and Kingston have been dominating together on the first squad for more than a year now, and I'm not even on the bench. Remus is not going anywhere, and I have to weigh my options. I want to play, that's all I want, Jude. If it be for Rogue, then it will be an even bigger dream come true. But I just want to be out on that pitch, showing the world what I can do. If it means being sold, especially to somewhere closer to Lara and Mason, then so be it."

A beat passes before he speaks. "I can't argue with that. If this game took me away from Aria, I mean ... I wouldn't allow it to. I couldn't have said that before I met her, but I understand it now. It will be the end of an era though, mate."

Sorrow swamps me, just like it has the other dozen times I've thought about my future in the sport of football. If I'm being honest, asking for a transfer or to be sold to another club has been on my mind for a year ... well before I found out about Mason. Living at the academy is a waste of my talent and time. I want to be loyal to the club that I moved up the ranks in, but they haven't shown me the same respect. And at the end of the day, I want to get out on that pitch.

If that can bring me closer to the woman I love and the child we made, that's two birds with one stone.

"It would be." I shake my head as my sister, Harlow, walks into the room. "Jude, mate, I've got to ring off. We'll talk soon, okay?"

"Go get what you want, brother," he says solemnly, and then I hang up.

"Smells delicious," Harlow says as she opens up the pot of sauce I have bubbling on the stovetop.

"Don't you go sticking any spoons in there. It's not ready, yet." I wag a finger at her and go back to chopping up garlic for the bread I'm about to pop in the oven.

"He's so picky about his prep," she teases.

Harlow is two years younger than I am and is currently attending university in London. Yet another member of my inner circle who resides in the city I desire to make it to. She's studying to be a nurse and is quite bright when she isn't stumbling home pissed at three in the morning. My sister is my exact opposite; an extroverted member of the secondary school pep squad, she has always loved being the center of attention. The more eyes on her, the more she thrives. Always the kind that strangers gravitate toward, she'll talk to absolutely anyone about anything for hours.

I admire my sister, but we're so different that sometimes I need a break from her. It's been a while, though, so my irritation meter is quite low at the moment.

"You didn't have to come home. It's just a casual drop in," I tell her.

Mum rang her when I told my parents I'd be coming home, and Harlow jumped on the next train. She told everyone it was because she was dying to see me, but I know better. If there is something Harlow doesn't want me or our parents to know, it's that she's homesick.

So I guess I can act a little kinder toward her this visit.

"And miss the Italian extravaganza? Not on your life." My sister's pearly white smile makes my lips imitate them on a smaller scale.

Harlow and I could be twins. We're the type of siblings who strangers never have to guess if we're related or not. Same almost-black hair, same inky dark eyes. Our mother's dimple in our left cheek, and the strong will of our father.

"Well, then if you're eating, you're helping. Set the table, please," I instruct her.

"You can't tell me what to do, you're not my dad!" She pretends to protest, but chuckles as she walks to the cabinet.

That sentence hits me square in the chest, so hard that I have to momentarily grab onto the island countertop, my knuckles going white. Thankfully, my sister is focused on the task at hand, and unaware of the major meltdown I'm trying to shake off.

Because while I'm not her father, I am *someone's* father—a fact that is still sinking into my bones.

Sooner or later, I'm going to have to share that fact with Harlow. And my parents. I dread the conversation; not only do I despise talking unnecessarily, but confrontation and deep discussions are my kryptonite.

As I move back to the stove, testing a strand of spaghetti to see if it's cooked, I resign myself to having a splendid dinner.

Life is about to become *loads* more complicated, my family can have one night of blissful obliviousness.

7

LARA

"Do you want blueberries in your pancake, darling?"

Louis stands in front of the stove in the Christmas pajamas I gave him last year, the ones with a snowy polar bear print. It's only October, but I know he's already in full holiday mode ... he's always been a sucker for Christmas.

"No, that's all right. I'm going to have a banana instead, thanks," I answer, rubbing the sleep out of my eyes.

Mason is already in his high chair, his chubby little cheeks covered in smashed strawberries and remnants of pancakes. Bending down, I kiss his dirty face, rubbing my nose against his.

This is how most weekend mornings go, with Louis up earlier than I am, making breakfast. Mason is an early riser, and I appreciate the Saturday and Sunday break when Louis gets up with him, as I'm the one who does all the morning preparation during the week.

Our flat is a block from the ocean, and we wake to the smell of salt hanging in the air daily. It's built in an old shipping warehouse, with the units boasting brick walls and open-beamed ceilings. I love this place and found it even before Louis and I became official. It was *just* in my price range as a struggling twenty-year-old mum to be, and I cut out a lot of my expenses to be able to afford it.

It's become a home in the past two years, one that we've all contributed to together. I've done most of the decorating, everything fitting into the seaside industrial theme as I like to call it. A lot of aquas and soft whites, paired with wrought iron and some more modern pieces. I've kept it comfortable, with overstuffed furniture, and tried to incorporate Mason's artwork on the fridge, or blown up in a deconstructed canvas over the sofa.

Louis was the one who fixed up the kitchen, buying us the appliances he claimed all good home chefs should use. He's the person who unclogs the shower drain and picks out the candles. I thought it was odd at first, a man wanting to fill our flat with candles, but he's so silly about it that it's become endearing.

"Hi, Mummy!" Mason coos in that sweet little voice of his, waving from his high chair.

I love that he is starting to speak, to tell me the things he wants or needs. Sometimes, I'll wake up to him on the baby monitor, singing in his crib. It jolts me every time, that this angelic little boy who I've raised from a tiny baby, is growing into a real human being with feelings and emotions.

"Hi, bub. How did you sleep?" I ask him, trying to speak to him like an adult.

I'm obsessed with those lousy parenting articles you find all over the Internet, from how to sleep train your child to preparing them for Mensa. Most of them are total rubbish, but I'm addicted. My latest opinionated find was how all mums should talk to their toddlers as if they were conversing with a thirty-year-old.

"Good!" Mason answers, smiling up at me with all of his baby teeth.

"And what are you eating here?" I ask, pointing to his tray, trying to get him to recall words from his memory.

"Straws and cakes!" my boy answers, shoving another piece of pancake in his mouth.

I ruffle his jet-black hair, and it makes me think of Vance. "Very good, love!"

Louis walks to the table, setting down my plate of pancake and bananas, and a cup of strong, inky tea. I can see where he's poured the milk, a cloud forming in the liquid. In a second he's back, with his own plate piled high with a mountain of pancakes and syrup.

I'm about to thank him, when the words that, without fail, send rage through my veins come out of his mouth.

"Just have to go have a smoke, yeah?" Louis is shrugging into his jacket, the one he wears on the balcony in the winter when he's lighting up.

We don't have many points of contention, but this is one of them. "Do you really need to do that now? We're sitting down to breakfast."

Louis's eyes grow irritated. "Breakfast that I cooked. Just give me a minute, Lar? Christ."

The door doesn't shut gently as he goes out to inhale that rubbish. As if smoking one of those electronic cigarettes won't likely give him cancer in the exact same way the old-fashioned ones do.

We've gotten in row after row about this. How unhealthy it is for him, for me, but especially for Mason. Why he can't just quit, since I ask very little of him. He, conversely, comes back swinging, throwing the fact that he has been here for me through a pregnancy that wasn't his.

Louis is a good man, but he, just like all people in the world, has his thorns. His temper when it comes to subjects he's pigheaded about can cut deeper than a knife.

When he finally comes back in, I don't feel an ounce guilty about lying to him.

"I have to take Mason out this morning." My heart ticks up a notch, because pulling the wool over someone's eyes will do that to you.

Louis cuts into his pancakes, the entire kitchen now reeking of smoke. "That's fine. I was going to log on and do some work anyway."

Another sticking point between us, I loathe that he brings his work home. Louis is an architect, actually a brilliant one, but it means late hours in the flat living room and random assignments that take him away from us. Part of me wants to pick a fight about this, but I'm getting off pretty easily while lying about bringing my son to meet his biological father.

Seemingly glazing over that situation, Louis speaks again. "I thought that caterer the other day was a good option. Have you started calling florists? What do you think you want for your bouquet?"

That gnawing feeling of dread is back, eating at my intestines. How can I sit here and have an honest conversation with him about wedding details, when the whole ordeal makes me want to throw up the pancake I just ate?

I have no idea what I think about that caterer, or what kind of flowers I want in my bouquet. Half the time, there is an alien sensation coming from my ring finger, because it's so wonky that a diamond ring is sitting on it.

Trying to inhale deeply without appearing as if I've just gone into a full-blown panic attack, I shrug. "We'll get to it."

Louis seems to take this answer in stride because there are no sidelong glances or questioning stares. He just stabs another piece of his breakfast, in a world oblivious to my doubts.

While on the other side of the table, I'm in a landslide of second thoughts.

The Mighty Anchor

The wind kicks up as I carry Mason into the park, the cold chafing his nose and turning it red.

I pull his hat down farther over his ears, and he tries to squirm away. "Walk! Mommy, walking!"

This is his demand for me to put him down, to let him stumble over the grass all by himself. When I agreed to the meeting, Vance had given me directions to a park just outside of Brighton. I know for a fact that it's for privacy, so no one in the area would see us together, or Vance meeting his son for the first time. I'm just not sure if it's for his sake or mine.

When Vance and I had been together, I'd been in my final year of secondary school. As a teenage girl going through her final year of school, I'd wanted to bring my boyfriend around my friends, hold hands on the front steps of school, bring him to dances, and the odd sports game.

He allowed none of that. When he came to Brighton, we spent the majority of our time together alone, either in his car, down on the beach, or in one of our separate houses. The brute hadn't wanted to share me, or at least that's the excuse he used most of the time. I'd been generally okay with that, seeing as I got limited time with him, but after a while, it got old. Having a relationship with someone who's as elusive and secretive as Vance was a job, not an enjoyment. Being with someone is supposed to enrich your life, not complicate it.

And that's what he had done. He made our connection something that was closed off from the world. I never met Jude or Kingston, the closest people to him aside from me. I felt like a shameful part of his life, even when he told me he loved me.

One of the final straws had been when I asked him to the twelfth year formal, and he declined. Told me it was a daft tradition, that he had more important things to focus on like his future and being the best keeper in all of England.

Vance Morley is dedicated to everything he does and everyone he feels deserves it. Except for me.

Perhaps it had been in his best interest to keep this under wraps ... Lord knows he's done it in the past.

"Thank you for driving all this way."

That gruff voice, the one that can still send cravings for him running through my veins, speaks at my back. I turn, and there he is in all of his Goliath glory. The wind-swept hair, the shade of midnight, and a gray wool coat that probably cost more than a few months' rent on my flat pulled around his muscled physique.

"It's better than meeting in Brighton." I nod curtly, because his stealth planning saves me a lot of trouble.

What would the community say if they knew Vance is the father of my son?

Since before Vance arrived, I set Mason on his feet. He's currently trying to chase a squirrel up a tree and giggling wildly in the process.

"My gosh, he's gotten bigger since I saw him. And that was only weeks ago," Vance mutters next to me.

"The child could eat me out of house and home. He requires a new pair of shoes practically every week." I chuckle, looking in the same direction as Vance, admiring my son.

Our son.

Suddenly, the man who used to hold my heart in his hands turns to me, a stricken look on his face.

"Whatever he needs, let me help you with it. I owe so much, I didn't know ..."

The organ in my chest, the one that wears a worn out tattoo of his name on it, practically cracks in half. I may harbor a lot of resentment, but you'd be a monster not to understand the emotions Vance is going through.

I lay a hand on his arm, and the warmth that spreads up my fingers makes my eyelids flutter closed for a second too long.

"You're right, you didn't know. There should, then, be no guilt on your part. I don't expect anything from you; I'm not struggling; it was merely a joke, a teasing gripe about parenthood. Vance, clearly, I'm not after your money. I hope you know I never was. Otherwise, wouldn't we be in a very different situation?"

We watch as Mason spins, his head tilted back, the sky his focal point. Without warning, he stops, the dizziness rushing to his head, and he almost topples over but catches himself at the last minute.

"The things that children find amusing." I shake my head.

"Why didn't you tell me? Truly, Lara, why?" His tone is the definition of hurt.

I sigh, trying to put my jumbled, frayed emotions in order. The answer is simple, though.

"I was heartbroken. You left me. When I decided to keep him, I told myself that he was mine. He's the one purely amazing thing that came out of the pain we caused each other. And that's what I've kept telling myself every day since he was born."

"And what do you tell yourself about us? What do you think about what I told you in the café?"

8

LARA

"And what do you tell yourself about us? What do you think about what I told you in the cafe?"

His words hang between us, the emotion of them vibrating through my chest. They catch me off guard, and as usual, I feel as if Vance Morley is always trying to one-up me.

Vance didn't want to bring me into his world, once upon a time, but I also never wanted to be a part of it. Yes, I fought him tooth and nail to bring me to fancy parties, or introduce me to his elite friends. For a time, I thought it would be fun to pretend that the upper-crust universe he was making a name for himself in could be my tier, too.

But in the end, I didn't want that life any more than he wanted to give it. I'm a homebody, a girl who grew up near the ocean in a small bungalow-style home with her single mother raising her. We never had much, and that had been all right. More than all right ... it was ace. I'm simple, with average tastes and no visions of grandeur. Most people in this world are looking for a way to have more, to get ahead, to come out on top.

Me? I'm content with a little space of my own, people who love me, and a job I rather like.

Even if Vance kept me hidden, making it a point not to bring me around his posh friends ... I hadn't wanted all that came with the life of an athlete's girl. Aside from the constant rat race to keep up with the other females trying to take your spot or compete with you, the lifestyle is one I didn't envy. Traveling all the time, staying up just to glimpse your man for twelve seconds before he had to leave again. Spending holidays alone, worrying about what he was doing on the road, the loneliness of being with a man who put his career before you. Eventually, I'd have had to raise a family on my own. How ironic that I ended up in the same lot.

"Vance, I'm engaged. To marry another man." Thrusting my hands out, I hope the body language conveys how ridiculous his earlier statement about winning me back is.

"Do you love him?" he fires back, catching me off guard again.

I nod slowly. "He's been there for me since before Mason was born."

One corner of Vance's mouth turns up, and I only know the bastard is smiling because that damn dimple winks at me. "That's not a declaration of undying devotion. You couldn't even tell me you were in love with the man. Which means you're not."

That statement feels like a bullet to the chest. I'm not accustomed to this version of Vance—the one that's almost cocky in demeanor. Self-assured, brutish, selfish—I don't know this man. Yes, he had some of these tendencies, but the boy I grew up across the street from was gentle and misunderstood.

"I do love him." I have to refrain from stamping my foot, my voice already giving away the slight pitch I'm using to convince myself of my words.

Vance shakes his head, a smirk gracing his lips, as if he knows I'm lying.

And that's when he steps toward me, neglecting all the laws of personal space and acceptable ex-boyfriend behavior.

"You've lied to me enough, it seems, so please don't lie anymore. That ring on your finger is making you all twitchy. Let's not do this. We're not naïve to the way the world ceases to exist when we're together."

I want to pound on his chest and scream, maybe rip his hair out. Or my own. Because he can't just do this. Come home and destroy everything I've so carefully constructed in my content little bubble.

My mind goes blank though, and I can do none of that, because Vance brings his hand to my cheek, cradling it in his palm. It's just a small touch, nowhere near the lengths and bounds we used to go to.

"You can't just waltz back into my life, say every romantic thing you've ever read in a book, and expect me to go weak at the knees," I whisper, but my feet won't move.

His hand is on my jaw, and I want so badly not to, but I lean into it. The roughness of his palm, the warmth of his hand, the sheer comfort of it makes me want to weep.

It's like coming home.

Vance, his embrace, his innate knowledge of me, the way his eyes hold everything we can't say ...

Blimey, it devastates me. It all hurtles into me like a car crash, something I want so badly to turn away from but I can't.

We're in a trance, one that's only broken when our son scrambles over, crying "Mummy!"

I jolt, backing away from Vance and his singular point of contact on my cheek as if he's burned me. My heart beats irregularly, like it's been taken out and put back, but not in the way it was supposed to be.

Vance's attention is no longer on me, but solely directed at the little boy peering up at us.

"Hi, Mason."

Vance's voice is husky with a knot of emotion, as if he's trying to talk past the lump in his throat.

Seeing them together, my son's father crouched down beside him, it's like looking in a mirror that predicts the future. Mason is Vance's twin, a much younger version of the burly, dark-featured man trying to foster a relationship with his child.

I have to blink back the tears in my eyes.

Vance clears his throat. "I'm ... Vance."

There was a pause there, as if he wanted to say more but thought better of it. I gulp, because I can't seem to move or talk. This moment is so precious, the first time they're speaking.

I've dreamed of this day for a long time, even if I've kept that ember burning in the back of my brain, for only me to cherish. Idly, I wonder what Louis would think of this, of his all but adopted son meeting his biological father for the first time. What mess have I created by opening this Pandora's box? Mason calls my fiancé Daddy.

"Vance!" Mason squeals, his fascination with saying people's names a new trick he's learning.

"That's right!" his father responds, and I swear I can feel the glee in his words, it's tangible. Vance pulls something out of his jacket. "I brought you a present."

"Present!" Mason yelps again, because he knows and loves that word. "Pwease!"

Vance glances up at me, a smile stretching his face so wide that I can't help but smile back. "The kid's got manners."

"Yes, he does." I ruffle my son's hair.

In his large hands, Vance holds a small football. Nothing near regulation size, but the Rogue Football Club logo is emblazoned on most of the hexagons and pentagons. He sets it down on the grass, between Mason and him.

"I'm not sure if you're a football man, but I am, so I thought

I'd teach you a little something. I'm going to pass it to you, and you pass it back."

Mason's entire body is vibrating with excitement, and I know it's because Vance just placed a ball at his feet. I won't share this with the man who is trying to wreck my world, but his son loves football. He has a tiny ball and goal at home that he punts into all day long.

"Okay, get ready, champ!" Vance crouches, so that he's not standing at full height, and gently kicks the ball to nestle at Mason's feet.

My son, his mocha eyes looking straight up at the matching pair, looks down at the ball and then back up. He's contemplative for a moment, the act of playing with this stranger something new entirely. Then, as if a lightbulb switches on in his mind, he grins his gap-tooth grin and winds his leg up.

Mason sends the football soaring, misdirectioned, back to Vance, who has to lunge out to get control of it with his foot. As if it's hard for him, he does this with all the grace of a jungle cat.

"*Goallll!* Great job, Mason!" Vance cries, and scoops my little guy up a in hug, lifting him off the ground.

Giggles burst from our son's throat, and I swear my ovaries explode from the cuteness overload.

I've thought a lot about what he would be like as a father. The Vance I knew then compared to the Vance playing with his son right now in front of me—they don't align. I thought Vance would be reserved, no-nonsense, and feared that if I did get him involved from the beginning of the baby's life, that he would fail miserably at loving the child.

How wrong I'd been. Vance is a natural ... anyone within a thousand-mile radius could feel the pure love radiating off of him. And if their small game of passing the football back and forth is any indication, Mason is taken with him, too.

He is his father's son. And I'm in for a world of trouble.

9

VANCE

"The cavalry has arrived!"

Kingston steps out of the white Rolls Royce he just drove into Brighton in, throwing his arms out as if this was a movie premier instead of he and Jude standing in my parent's driveway.

"Bloody hell, if I'm forced to listen to one more minute of two thousands rap ..." Jude snarls, rubbing at his temples.

"What's that, old man? The ball and chain making you a dull bloke?" Kingston slaps him on the back and then moves to wrap me in a bear hug.

Both Kingston and Jude are engaged to the women they met while we were all still, mostly, in the academy together. Aria, Jude's fiancée, is a recording artist with killer pipes and a best-selling album. I relate to her, but we've never connected much. Like me, Aria came from nothing and worked tooth and nail to get where she is now.

Poppy, on the other hand, is an international model who verbally bitch slapped Kingston the first time they ever met. I was there; it was glorious. Since they've gotten together, she's come out as one of the assault victims of a famous photographer who is now behind bars. She and Kingston have a lot in common, and I'm happy that they've had each other to get through some difficult times in the past year.

"You still can't pick me up, it never works." I grunt as he tries to haul me off the ground.

"I've been slaying it in the gym. Dammit, I thought I would finally be able to do it," Kingston protests as he moves away from me, huffing.

It's been a running joke for years, his inability to lift me off my feet. "You're simply no match."

"Yeah, with your superhuman bones and Hagrid-like stature," Jude jokes and they follow me into the house.

When they mentioned coming down to see me for a night, I protested. I have serious ground to make up here. But, they insisted, and per usual, I relented. Now that they're here, spending the night at my parent's place, I'm almost glad I let them wear me down. I've been in a pit of despair, stressing over all the decisions hanging over my head, and having my best mates here to cheer me up seems to be doing the trick.

I chuckle. "I see Aria still has you reading Harry Potter?"

Kingston elbows me. "If he doesn't read a chapter a night, she doesn't give up the goods. I'd read eight if it meant Poppy would give me more time between the sheets. Blimey, that woman is a goddess."

"You're one randy bastard. The other day she could hardly walk." Jude scoffs.

Kingston pats himself on his own back. "What can I say, she does it for me."

"I think it's splendid you're finally pulling off the caveman mask and actually indulging in an activity that requires brain power." I smirk at Jude.

Back in academy, it was all I could do to drag them to our

classes. They were mandatory, of course, since we lived our life for football and forewent traditional education. Throughout what would have been our primary and secondary schooling years, we were required to take the same curriculum on the Rogue campus. Kingston and Jude could have cared less if they ever learned multiplication tables ... all they cared for was getting out onto the pitch.

Since football consumed me too, I couldn't argue with that. But I was always the one of us who actually took pride in my schoolwork and found it interesting. While those two schemed how to sneak out of the dorms and down to the pub in Clavering, I laid on our couch with paperback versions of classic novels. I taught myself division and geometry and memorized the events of World War I, not only so I could relay that information to my mates and keep their grades in good standing, but because I truly enjoy learning.

"Oh, right, I forgot, you read for fun, too. I don't understand that." Kingston shakes his head, pretending to be disappointed in me.

"What book are you on? Who is your favorite character?" Not wanting to spook Jude, I shrug as if his answer doesn't matter.

In reality, I've been waiting almost twelve years for either of my best friends to become Potterheads, and am giddy that I'll finally have someone to discuss the books with.

Waving his hands in a ceasing motion, Kingston intervenes. "No, no, I outlaw that. No nerd talk, we're here on a mission and reading will only take us off course."

I have to admit, I've missed them. Our personalities mesh well together; Kingston is the showboat, the outgoing obnoxious one who keeps us light and laughing. Jude is the alpha, the pretty boy with a golden foot. And I'm the backbone, the silent, guiding glue that keeps us moving and supported.

"You worked out at Brighton, eh?" Kingston gives me a side-eye glance.

Is this the mission he's here on? To get reconnaissance on my feelings about football clubs? Because right now, it's the last thing on my mind.

"Yes. So?" I roll my eyes, but I've missed his ribbings.

Jude clears his throat. "Niles got word of it ... I don't think he's happy about that, mate."

Ire leaves a bitter taste in my mouth. "I don't bloody well care about his happiness, mate. This is a man who has, time and time again, passed me over. He can't say shite about me conditioning at another facility, alone I might add, when he does nothing but leave me sitting in the academy."

They're both silent for a moment, and then Kingston doubles over laughing. "There's the mean old grump I've been waiting for. Good to see you, Vance, glad you're back. And you're right, fuck him. I mean, I respect the guy and he literally owns my bollocks, but out of the three of us, he's done you the dirtiest. And he sent me to football Siberia, so that's saying a lot. Do whatever you want, brother."

I nod, not knowing what else to add to the conversation.

"Do you want to play here? I mean, I just thought you'd end up playing with us for Rogue in London. That was the plan." Jude still sounds bummed about the revelation that I may not join them.

"And that's why you're the dreamer of us," I tell him, slapping him on the shoulder. "But it's time to wake up. I'm twenty bloody two; time is wasting away. And I have other things to consider now."

My two best mates exchange a look, and Kingston is the one to touch the elephant sitting in the room. "When do we get to meet her? And him?"

Ah, I understand now. They're here to vet Lara and Mason.

Well, that *is* on my mind—the only thing on my mind. It's only been two days since our secret meeting in the park, the one outside Brighton that I'd found so Lara wouldn't be uncomfortable. If it were up to me, I would have met her and our son on the bloody beach that we'd first fallen in love on, for all the world to see. I want to shout from the rooftops that Mason is my child, but I know it's more complicated than that. Lara needs time to process, to digest the things I'm telling her. So, I agreed to speak to my son for the first time in a location outside of our hometown.

In the first week since I'd been back in Brighton, I've seen Lara twice, and Mason once. I spilled my heart to her, told her everything I've been bottling up since the initial discovery that I have a son. Everything I could possibly do thus far to get the woman I love, and my family, back well, I've done it. I've warred with myself about my future in football, and if need be,

I'll walk away.

That's how hard this has all hit me. I was a bastard once, giving up on her because of the game I love. I won't do it again.

But I won't walk away from my son. Just thinking about him, my little mini-me, and the way his smile lights up his entire face. How small his hand had been in mine when he'd taken the small football from me. The way his energy powers the world around him, when his little legs carried him across the grass. I hear his laughter in my ears all the time now.

I can't stand the thought of not being his father, of not having him in my life.

"I'm not sure, mate. I have one week left to convince her I'm worth complicating her entire life. Popping up unexpectedly with you two arseholes might throw a wrench in it."

"Mate, we don't care. You kept her hidden long enough. It's time for us to be uncles." Jude nods at me, solemnly.

I blow out a sigh. "It's not that simple. She's engaged to

someone else, and I just found out that no one in Brighton knows I'm Mason's father."

"Wait, she hasn't told anyone that you're the daddy? Your parents don't know?" The octave of Kingston's voice reaches new heights with every word uttered.

"What the bloody hell?" Jude says at exactly the same time. "So, she lied to you about having a son for a year and a half, and now, come to find out, she's lied to everyone else, too? That bitch—"

"Enough," I roar. I point at Jude, "You won't talk about Lara like that. Neither of you will, or I'll break your kicking foot."

"Harsh, mate," Kingston curses under his breath.

"I'm not pleased with her actions ... bloody hell, I'm furious. But, I never told you the entire story. When we were together, it wasn't our schedules that kept me from bringing her around. It wasn't her commitment issues that barred her from meeting you. It was me. I kept her a secret, kept our relationship this private thing with ridiculous rules. Lara is somewhat justified in all she's done, and she did it to protect her son. If I can forgive that and look past it, you will too."

They both look stunned, their jaws slack and wobbling.

"Shite, you're really in love with this bird." Jude's expression goes from somber to smirking in half a second.

"And you're a wanker for keeping her away from us. I can't believe you, Vance!" Kingston smacks my pec, as if he's anyone to talk about respecting females.

"There is no keeping us away now. Take us to her. It's time we meet." Jude stamps his foot like a petulant child.

"Mate, she's working. She's a teacher." A fact I found out from some extensive Internet sleuthing.

"I don't care. If you don't take us, we'll cause chaos around town trying to find her. Poor fiancé, we're about to turn his world to shite." Kingston grins that devilish grin he gets when he's about to pull a prank.

Immediately, I grab my coat from where it hangs on the back of a chair. "Fine, I'll take you. But you have to promise to behave."

Jude nods. "Fine. But on the way, you're telling us more about exactly what went down between you two. I think I may need to teach you about the art of wooing."

10

LARA

Slumped over my desk, I re-read, for the fifth time, a sentence one of my students wrote.

No one tells you, when you get into education, that this is some of the hardest work. I love working with young minds, discussing with them and teaching on a personal level in the classroom. But the grading, the endless nights of checking tests and correcting mistakes long after putting Mason down for bed, this is the part of my job that I despise.

It's mindless and lonely, and while I do enjoy reading the thoughts and inner-workings of my student's brains, there are some papers that just flat-out miss the mark. Case in point, this theory on David Copperfield being an undercover Russian spy. I want to roll my eyes at every other word.

My classroom door bangs against the back wall, and my head whips up, the noise jolting me from my lackadaisical focus.

"Is it time for a martini yet?"

Stefania strolls into my classroom, her inky black hair making an entrance of its own. My best mate at work started around the same time I did, transferring to Brighton from her home country of Spain simply because she was bored and wanted to branch out. That was Stef for you, impulsive, aggressively beautiful, and incapable of being tied down. She's like the sand beneath the shoreline in our town; just when you think you have her, she slips through your fingers.

At least, with men, she seems to adopt that method. As a friend, she is splendid. My babysitter when I need her, my shoulder when the tears came, and my drinking partner on the rare night off from motherhood.

"I have to get home. Louis wants to discuss wedding plans." I try to keep the anxiety from creeping into my voice.

"When are you going to dump that dodgy bloke?" She pretends to cringe.

"Bugger off, that's my fiancé." I chuckle, refraining from flipping up my middle finger at her.

Stef has never warmed to Louis. She says there is something wonky about him, that she could sense his aura or feel his spirit. Some shite she was peddling about knowing these things in her bones, having had ancestors who were witch doctors. I think she's simply a commitment-phobe who wants one of her only friends in town to be single and ready for a pint or a night dancing at the drop of a hat.

"For now." She tips her head and winks. "Anyways, come have a drink with me first. I don't think I can stand one more minute of grading inaccurate maths solutions."

The advanced calculus teacher, Stef has a penchant for being one of the coolest staff members in school. She makes her class interesting in a way I never thought maths could be, and she's bloody brilliant to boot.

Looking at the clock ticking on the wall behind my desk, I estimate that I have a good twenty-minute cushion to my arrival at home. I can run down the street with Stef, gulp down some liquid numbing, and then head home ... possibly more relaxed to talk about walking down the aisle and everything that comes before it.

"All right, fine. But you have to hear my complaints, and promise not to pressure me into two drinks. I do not want to be hungover for first bell tomorrow."

"I have never met a twenty-two-year-old who didn't wish for a hangover or more drinks. You're truly special, *mi amor*."

Gathering my things, I follow Stef out to the street, the constant soundtrack of my life, the ocean lapping the shore, playing in the background.

"Am I playing wingwoman tonight?" I chuckle, trying to test her mood.

More than once, I've acted as Stef's buffer or her pimp. There are nights when she feels like taking a man home, and other times where she's cursed and shunned all men to the devil. She likes to tell me it depends on the position of the moon and mercury, but I like to think it depends on her drink count and menstrual cycle.

"If the right man comes along, I may need your flirting assistance." A sly grin is thrown my way.

It's an inside joke between us, my flirt training her. Unlike so many of my peers, I never truly experienced a twenty-something life. I went from hiding my relationship in high school, to clawing my way out from under my parent's roof to raise a baby on my own. I didn't get the self-discovery phase, or the single, wild period. With Stef, and our odd night out, I get to let my hair down and forget about all the sacrifices I've made.

And so ... I flirt through her. I tell her what I would do or say if a stranger approached me in a pub or club, and she acts it out. It's a game for me, living vicariously through her.

It also assuages my guilt that I'm out on the town, wondering what it would feel like if someone other than Louis took interest.

"Um, is that Jude Davies?" Stef stops dead, leaving me to

walk by myself until I look back to realize she is no longer with me.

Following her gaze, I land on three massive figures across the street. Brighton Secondary School is on the main road in Brighton. Not close to the shops, but farther down the road where only a couple of storefronts and eateries exist. It's rare for this part of town to be crowded, and the pub we frequent is a teacher's spot.

But sure enough, Vance is staring at me from the pavement, Jude Davies and Kingston Phillips flanking him.

"*Bloody hell,*" I mutter, all of my organs twisting into knots.

My heart ricochets against my ribs, my stomach drops to my feet. I have to consciously press my hands at my sides to keep from smoothing my hair or pulling my sunglasses off my face.

"Am I dreaming? Is this a fantasy? Because I told you if the right man came along, I'd need help, and now it looks like the three horsemen of the apocalypse arrived and my knickers just croaked." Stef is actively laughing, as if this situation can't even be reality.

"No, it's real all right. Unfortunately, they're not here for the apocalypse. Just for my head." My jaw clicks as I grind my teeth together.

"What is going on?" My friend gapes at me but follows as I cross the street to meet my fate.

Ignoring her question, I march straight up to Vance. "You really hunted me down at my place of work?"

His lips twitch, as if this whole thing is mildly hilarious, but those chocolate brown eyes are serious. And, of course, he doesn't answer the questions but opts for silence.

"Hey, I'm Kingston. Heard a lot about you, and don't nag him. This was my idea, so blame me. Just don't kick me in the bollocks, or my kicking foot. Vance already threatened that, and I'm prepared."

Kingston Phillips, England's richest playboy and prankster, steps forward to extend his hand to me.

Stef starts to giggle beside me, and I know why. This is ludicrous. "Do you *know* them?"

I guess a lot of the full-time residents in Brighton, and many people I grew up with, don't know of my connection to Vance. First off, we kept it under wraps, so why would they? But he also didn't live here for much of his childhood. Yes, residents always touted this as the place he came from, but truth be told, Vance never spent a lot of time here.

"Sort of," I address her, humiliated that they tracked me down and stunned that this is the way I am meeting his best mates for the first time.

I also have no idea what I am going to tell Stefania, but I suppose she's the best person for this to happen in front of if it had to be anyone.

"It's nice to meet you. Why don't we go inside and sit down? A pint might take the edge off all of this."

Just like that, Jude Davies, the pride of Britain's football empire, was escorting me into my local pub to grab a bite.

11

LARA

"When I woke up today, I never thought in a million years that my day would end like this."

Stef is still in a state of hypnotic hysteria, and I almost want to snap my fingers in front of her face. How many times have I played it cool for her in front of men? Lesson learned, she cannot return the favor.

"This is Stefania, she teaches maths at our school. And apparently, is an undercover football fan." My tone is all sarcasm.

We've never talked about sports, so I suppose I'm surprised at her reaction to the men sitting in a dingy, wooden booth across from us at the Brighton Blue Craw Pub.

"Pleasure to meet you." Kingston winks at her.

It's no secret he's engaged, to the most famous supermodel in the world, obviously. The news was splashed across every tabloid and website in circulation. But apparently, he's still a charming bugger and it shows. Because next to me, Stef sighs like one of those fainting damsels in a historical romance novel.

Vance has still not taken his eyes off of me, as we sit directly across from one another in the innermost section of the booth.

Every hair follicle prickles with awareness, and I have to clench my thighs to keep from having the reaction my body so clearly wants me to have toward him.

We've exchanged messages a few times since his meeting Mason formally for the first time, and I know we have a lot to discuss. I just ... don't want to. I'm terrified of what he'll say, what he'll profess this time. Will he want to make things legal? A custody arrangement? My soul trembles with fear every time I think of it. Having to ship Mason off to wherever he's playing for days at a time? I could break down into sobs right now just thinking about it.

Then Kingston turns to me. "I'm so glad we finally get to meet. I apologize on behalf of our daft giant here; it should have been a long time ago."

I can't help but laugh at that. "As if I have much choice now."

"You've got me there. I should have been paying more attention back then, but unfortunately, I was a wanker."

"Some would say you still are." Vance finally breaks his silence.

"Valid point. But now I'm a wanker with a conscience," Kingston concedes.

"Now I understand what Vance meant when he said you are a smooth talker." I pull a memory out of my brain, the image tinged with rose-tinted frames.

Even if he wouldn't bring me around to meet them, Vance talked about his two friends all the time when we were together.

Stef eyes me like I'm in big trouble for not disclosing all the facts of my past to her, and I wave her off. *Not right now*, I try to say with my glance, *but soon I'll tell you.*

Jude is pretending to glance at a menu, but what he's truly doing is giving me a once-over. He's assessing me, not in a sexual way, but in a protective way. Protective of his friend.

Despite fighting the feeling, it warms my heart. Vance

The Mighty Anchor

doesn't allow many people close to him, but he allowed these two to worm their way in. They look out for each other, and I know without knowing that he's confessed many things to his friends about me. What I'd give to pick Kingston's brain.

It occurs to me that these three lived a life together that not many people ever get to experience. Jet setting, endless amounts of money, exclusive parties, free merchandise ... anything they wanted was within reach.

I've seen him on the cover of magazines, in paparazzi photos on Instagram, on the telly when the celebrity news portion of the morning show came on. Vance has been with a fair share of different women since we split, the leggy models draping off his arm like beautiful accessories. I wonder what his friends think of me, this dull girl from a nowhere town. I'm not London chic, I don't come from posh society.

"You're a tough bird; I like that." Kingston pats my hand in a friendly gesture.

For the first time since I spotted them on the street, I relax marginally.

"I'd also really love a Guinness and some chips. We staked out your school for about an hour, I'm starving." Kingston pats his washboard stomach.

Stef almost chokes on the martini she procured out of thin air. How did she get a drink but none of the people at the table who really need liquid courage right now received any handouts?

"What subject do you teach?" Jude asks, his eyes holding judgment.

The waitress, Nelly, walks up to our table and asks for our orders before I can answer. She looks starstruck, as do many other patrons in the pub, but doesn't have the courage to take it further than that. Even if they weren't three of the most famous athletes in England, these men would attract attention. Devilishly handsome, the lot of them, and freakishly muscled and large in stature ... there is no subtle magnetism to them. Their pull is like being thrown against a wall.

There is no way my coworkers aren't going to hear about this. As it is, I spot two of them whispering in our direction from the other side of the pub. There will be questions after this, and my rage at Vance grows as swiftly as a tsunami. I can't prepare for it, but it swamps me, drowning me in the feeling that, soon, everyone will know who the father of my son is.

When she walks away with our drink order, and the men's ridiculous food order, I turn back to Jude.

"I teach English." My answer is short and to the point.

He seems to weigh my words. "Have you ever read Harry Potter?"

My lips split into a smile. "Of course I have. Would I be a teacher from England who tells her students to read if I hadn't read one of the greatest series of all times? By a British author, not to mention."

Jude nods. "I find that answer acceptable. And you live in Brighton?"

"In a flat I rent all on my own. Any other questions? Do you want to see my medical history or credit score?" Cheeky is my defense setting.

Kingston snorts, foam from his beer splashing onto his hand. "I more than like you, Lara."

Our conversation ventures into surface-level small talk, with Stef taking the reins. She and Kingston hold up the heavy end of the discussion, talking about anything and nothing at all. Jude asks about my job some more, and I inquire about their academy days, just for something less awkward to talk about. Though Stef doesn't know it, we're all skirting around the elephant in the room. No one wants to touch my relationship with Vance, or our son, with a ten-foot pole.

Vance is mute, his gaze roaming my body and face the entire time. I'm not sure if I want to scream at him or bloody throw myself across the table into his lap.

My drink is nearly empty when a cuckoo clock over the bar chimes the hour, and I'm roused from the spell of this delirious encounter.

"I have to get home." I attempt to scoot over, trying to make Stef let me out of the booth.

I'm already past my twenty-minute cushion by double, and I'm sure there are a couple of missed text messages and calls from Louis on my mobile.

"Can I talk to you?" Vance's deep growl shocks me.

It's the first thing he's said to me all night, and *now* is when he finds it convenient to request an audience?

My heart takes over, silencing the rational part of my brain that's about to answer no. "Yes."

What is wrong with me? Everyone shifts, scooting out of the booth to let he and I out. Vance motions me toward the hallway in the back, one I know leads to the toilets. I guess he's looking for what little privacy this place offers.

I shouldn't follow him, but my legs, body, and mind are useless.

After all this time, I'm still impervious to the power he has over me.

12

VANCE

In my entire life, I never expected to be sitting around a table at a pub with Lara, Jude, and Kingston.

Conversing and extroversion aren't my strong suits, which is why I stayed silent for almost the entire thing. Until Lara decided it was time to leave, and I knew I had to make another plea.

My leave in Brighton is halfway through, and I need to impress upon her my intentions. Aside from the possibility of us, I need her to know that I'm not going anywhere when it comes to Mason.

We stand in the hallway to the loo, each of our backs resting against the opposite walls, assessing each other.

"Never how I thought I'd meet your friends," she starts, crossing her arms over her chest.

The motion highlights the swell of her tits under her sweater, and I can't help the twitch of my eager cock. It's been so long since I've been with a woman, though none of them ever compared to her.

Giving my head a shake to clear it, I address her. "They wanted to meet you, I apologize if it felt like an ambush."

"So, it wasn't your idea. Why does that not surprise me?" Her voice takes on a tone of hurt and mocking.

"What is that supposed to mean?" I push her.

Lara rolls those gorgeous aquamarine eyes. "Come on, Vance. You never wanted me to meet them back when we were together. You always shrugged off my efforts to get to know them, and not once did you jump at the chance to bring me around your friends. In fact, it felt like you actively kept me hidden away like you were ashamed of how your posh football mates would view me."

If I wasn't staring at her with my own two eyes, I swear I'd think she'd just blown my head clear off from the sheer preposterousness.

"What the bloody hell are you talking about? We only had precious hours together when I was able to get away and see you! I didn't want to waste them hanging around with those two idiots. I wanted you all to myself. I didn't care what anyone else thought. Though for the record, you're lightyears above whatever preconceived notions you have about those two out there. You're more intelligent, stronger, braver, more beautiful, more captivating than any woman they've ever tried to chat up. I only cared what you thought. I still do."

She blinks, stunned. "Why do you do this? Freeze me out until the very last second and then attack me with these heart-crushing, spirit-lifting speeches. Damn you, Vance."

"I can't seem to act rationally around you. You send my frequency dial to haywire."

Blond locks, the color of spun golden silk, shake around her face as she twists her head gently from side to side, seeming to disagree with me. Whatever she feels, I have to make the point I originally brought her back here for.

"I have one more week here, Lara. I've given you space, but now we need to discuss how this is going to work. Mason is my son, and I want to be a part of his life. I want to be in his life. I want to tell my family, I want the world to know. I want to—"

She cuts me off, irate. "You've seen him for all of an hour, Vance. You don't know what you want, or how difficult it is to be a parent."

I try to breathe through the fury. "You're right, I don't. But I want more than anything to know. And don't throw that shite at me, you fell in love with him the first time you saw him. I don't need to have been around for his birth to know that. It's evident in every touch you share, in the way you look at him. I experienced that when I saw you on Main Street, before you even confirmed he was my son. It's innate. I love him."

"He has a father, Vance. One he calls Daddy. One who gets him out of his crib in the morning and feeds him dinner. Who rocked him to sleep when he was teething. You can't be there every day for him. He doesn't even know you."

"Because you didn't let him!" I yell, my voice a thunderclap.

Rage splinters in my cells, and there she is, twisting that fucking ring around her the fourth finger on her left hand.

"You didn't let me know him, or him me. This replacement came along and you're bloody pretending right through your picture-perfect life. It's all a sham."

"You have no idea what you're talking about." Unshed tears stain her voice.

I'm not sure how this conversation veered so far off the rails, but perhaps it's because I don't converse well. I'm loyal and steadfast, but when I state out loud that I want something a certain way, I'm stubborn. If I don't get it, when I don't ask for much, all hell breaks loose inside me.

In this case, I want Lara and our child with such a terrible yearning, that I'm crazed. I'm a wild beast, grunting and pounding my chest in a show of dominance. I can't help it.

"I don't know why you're going along with this, Lara. You don't love him." My words tremble in my throat.

Watching her wear another man's ring, plan her wedding with him, it's more than I can bear now.

"I've been a daft, blind fool up until this point, and I know I don't deserve you. But I don't care, because that's what love is. Love isn't patient or kind or all the other shite they always say it is. Love is swift and lethal, it has no regard for the emotions of its victims. I can't choose not to be in love with you. I tried to ignore it for a while, and that was shattered when I saw you on the street with our son. You don't love that man, you love *me*. And I sure as bloody hell am in love with you."

It feels like an anvil drops on my chest, and lifts off, at exactly the same moment. Like two trains collide right into me, and it's the most freeing feeling in the world. I've been struggling through this, trying to wade through muddy waters, but it's all so clear now.

"Vance, stop it, this is insanity ..." She breaks off on a sob, and although she's saying those things, Lara steps toward me, her petite body almost pressed against mine.

"You don't think I know that? You don't think I want to be the better man here, to walk away? I've lived my life to be that man, Lara. To stay loyal, to toe the party line. I walked away from you two years ago because I thought I was doing both of us a favor. I thought it would hurt less than staying. You don't think I want to stop this pain? Of course, I do. I just can't."

A beat passes, with both of us staring holes into the other's eyes.

And then, at the exact moment I reach for her, she pushes up on her toes. Our mouths meet in the middle, and the rest of the world explodes around us, leaving nothing but our two bodies intertwined.

Pushing her back until the base of her skull meets the wall, I devour her. Nothing slow or gentle about it, we're all lips and tongues and hands searching every surface of each other ... all the parts we've missed in the last two years.

My hands dive into her hair, the silk skimming past my fingertips, angling her head so I can push my tongue deeper into her mouth. I can barely breathe, sacrificing oxygen to taste more of Lara.

She sets my soul on fire, blazing a path straight from my brain all the way down to my toes. I smell her scent, that cinnamon and warm vanilla, and I just want to curl up around her.

I want to kiss her fast, kiss her slow, snog her until we're both delirious and the power of speech leaves us. The power to wound each other with words will cease to exist.

Lara makes tiny mewling sounds into my mouth, giving it back as good as she's getting. Her fingers have disappeared somewhere under the hem of my sweater, traveling the path of my happy trail up and down my abs. She's made me rock-solid in a matter of milliseconds, and I don't care who's watching because I'd take her right against this wall if she'll let it happen.

Like I told her, she makes me insane. And I can't stop it.

Behind one of the closed doors of the toilets, a sink goes on, the faint sound of whooshing water invading the heavy snogging session happening just out of my mate's vision. It seems to rouse Lara, and she pushes me back, shoving with all her might.

I'm a lust-crazed hunter, and I make a move to step back into my prey's personal space. But Lara sticks her arms out, blocking me from moving any farther. Her eyes are filled with horror, and she's rooted to the spot.

In that one glance, my heart rots ... because I know she's about to take back everything that just happened.

"You made a cheater out of me." She gasps, speaking past the hand covering her lips.

"Lara, no, that's not what—" I seem to trip over my words, my brain hazed over from her lips and tongue.

"Don't."

Just one word, and a slice of her cutting eyes, and then she's shouldering past me.

I hear the jingle over the door as she leaves, the scene out of sight in this back hallway of the quaint pub.

As much as that may have set me back, I don't regret it. Leaning against the wall, trying to catch my breath and my sanity, I know for a fact I would do it all over again.

Because I know, from the weight of her lips on mine and the desperation in her bones, that she still loves me.

13

LARA

The radio in my car hums an old Cyndi Lauper tune as I sit and stare at the dashboard absentmindedly.

I can't seem to get out of the bloody vehicle, to remove my keys from the ignition and start up the stairs to my flat. A screw inside my brain, or maybe my heart, has knocked loose and I'm not the same woman I was just twenty minutes earlier.

No, this woman trapped in the prison of her own body, in her own car, is a cheater. A goddamn adulterer who just betrayed everything she's worked to build.

Of anything I've ever tried to be, honest is the single biggest thing I strive for.

Growing up, my parents had a very unconventional relationship. I am an only child of divorced spouses, who were decent enough to each other that it almost seemed like I had one complete family. My mother and father were headed for a split before I even left my mother's womb, and by the time I turned two, they were legally separated. I grew up in a small one-floor home with my mother and saw my father on weekends or for school events or dance recitals. He was around as much as he could be, and my mum is a warrior who sacrificed for me.

But the one thing they instilled in me, taught me from an early age, was how to be honest. My parents spoke to me like an adult, telling me the truth in every situation we found ourselves in. They didn't sugarcoat that they no longer loved each other and served it to me straight. When I asked my mother about sex or drugs or falling in love, she would never gloss over the answer with kid gloves.

So, I've approached most of my life with honesty.

Funny, then, how Vance Morley seems to be my lie. Every. Single. Time.

I lied to everyone about our relationship. I lied by omission, to him, about getting pregnant. I lied to everyone about who Mason's father is ... or I guess I never had to because I just kept it a secret.

And now, I have to walk into the flat I share with my fiancé and completely lie to his face.

The gnawing feeling of dread, guilt, and shame boils in my gut, turning my insides to churning nausea. I want to sink into the floor, to just disappear into the earth so I don't have to face this.

Do I tell Louis? Do I pretend it never happened?

Of course, I can't pretend that. I've not been able to wipe the taste of Vance off my mouth no matter how many breath mints I popped on the way home. There is no way I will ever forget the searing brand he's left on my soul.

How am I going to marry Louis after this?

"If you're lost, you can look and you will find me, time after time," Cyndi Lauper sings, and the words hit me like a bullet.

My head is a mess, confusion and chaos running amok. But

if I don't go inside soon, I'll miss Mason's bedtime. And no matter how much of a disaster I am, my son deserves all the attention and love I can give him.

Slowly, I make my way out of the car, up the short pavement to the outside stairs leading to our front door, and unlock it.

"Mummy!" Mason crashes into me the second I walk through the door.

Instantly, all of my worries and regrets are put on hold. The warmth of his little arms wrapping around my leg in a genuine hug are all I need to focus on something other than my epic mistake not an hour earlier.

It takes forty-five minutes to get him to sleep, what with his nighttime bath, sippy cup of milk, song, and book routine and a ton of kisses from Louis and me. Even though I won't get to see him until morning, putting Mason to bed is one of my favorite activities of the whole day. He's no longer a baby, but more of a little boy now, and the sundown hours are the only time he'll let me cuddle him anymore.

"I got you an early wedding present." Louis wraps me in his arms as we walk back to the living room from the nursery, and something inside me feels empty.

"What's that?" I try to feign pleasant surprise, because if you act like you're happy than it ought to come true, right?

He nuzzles into my neck. "I threw out my last supply of e-cigarettes." As if it's the biggest accomplishment in the world, Louis pulls away and reveals the large white patch on his arm. "I'm quitting smoking. For our big day. For you."

And my stomach drops. Because less than two hours ago, I had another man's lips on mine. I had Vance's hands in my hair, half-blind with lust.

Here was Louis, giving up something so selflessly so that I'd be happy, and I cheated on him.

I feel rotten, right down to my core.

"That's wonderful, Louis. But I want to make sure you're doing it for you, and not me." Because if this all goes south, would that be something I ruined for him, too?

That right there, that seed of doubt Vance planted ...

No. Vance didn't plant that. It has existed in my heart from the moment Louis had gotten down on one knee. If I was being honest, which is apparently rare for me these days, it was there when I allowed him to hold Mason in the hospital.

I knew from the start that Louis, as good a man as he is, isn't the love of my life. He doesn't shatter my world.

But maybe that's overrated. I have a good thing going, it's stable and solid. My son is happy. When I think about a life with Vance, all I see is turmoil.

"I want to do everything for you," Louis answers, kissing my forehead.

As much as I feel that invisible scarlet *A* creeping out over my breastbone, I lean into it, willing myself to be happy at this moment.

The next morning, I head to my mum's house.

She still lives in the old neighborhood, in her one-floor single-family home. It's small and quaint, but she keeps the place clean and doesn't need much more than that. Mum is a petite dynamo, a quiet but hard-willed woman who never complains and keeps her nose to the grindstone. Perhaps it's why I've been able to survive everything I've been through; because my mother taught me how to control my life in the face of terrible odds.

After removing Mason from his car seat, he wriggles out of my arms and stumbles up to Mum's front steps, climbing on his hands and knees all the way up them. Before heading there myself, I turn and let my eyes roam over the house across the street.

The one the Morley's used to live in.

Now, a family of five live there, their children around the primary and secondary school ages. I don't know their names, and no one is outside at the moment. I swear, I can still picture Vance's shiny BMW he drove, in the first year he got his license, pulling into the driveway. We'd been nothing, back then, and my heart flipped over like an engine starting as he unfolded his long limbs out of the vehicle.

"My boy!"

Mum's greeting snaps me out of my haze, and I grab my nappy bag to join the two of them on the front steps.

"Hi, Mum." I wave, walking up just as she plucks Mason from the stairs and settles him on her hip.

Apparently, being her child meant tough love ... but being her grandchild means spoiling to the nth degree. Not that I can complain, she's a wonderful granny. Mason adores her, and she never protests if I ask her to watch him.

Like today, when I need an afternoon to just sit and think. Louis thinks we're visiting my mum for lunch and playing on the new tricycle she bought him. Yet again, I've lied.

Lying awake for all but an hour of the night before, I knew I needed to get my head straight. To think long and hard about what I am doing, where my life is going. What the hell that kiss means ...

I can count on my mother to watch my son and keep my absence from the visit under wraps if Louis asks. The only thing is, I still have to ask her to do that.

"Thanks for taking him for a little while," I say, dropping Mason's bag full of toys, food, and a change of clothes on her kitchen counter.

My son is already happily throwing things out of the toy box Mum keeps in her living room specifically for him. She watches on, balanced on the steps between her kitchen and sunken living room, smiling.

"It's no problem at all. He's a blessing, and as much time as I can have with him, I'll take it."

Trying to distract myself from the awkward question at hand, I begin pulling out Mason's snacks and sticking them in her refrigerator.

"Mum, if Louis asks, would you tell him I stayed the whole visit?" I hope my voice comes off as nonchalant, but it sounds too high in my ears.

I see her bristle as she turns to me. "I can do that."

Typical Mum, keeping a straight face and agreeing to whatever it is I need, but not without an air of curiosity smothering me. It's that type of mother's intuition, with a side of guilt, that makes children want to spill even their worst of offenses without being prodded.

"It's just ... I told him I was having lunch with you. And I don't want him to realize I didn't."

She nods, her face impassive. "I understand. I can tell him that if he does ask me."

Jesus, my heart is racing. I can't help blurting it from my mouth, although I attempt to keep my voice down if this is the one time in a thousand that Mason actually decides to listen to Mummy.

"I just have a lot of things I need to think about and need some time alone." Lest she thinks I'm having an affair or going to buy out the bar by myself.

"I've had those days." Her answer is still just as measured, just as un-seeking.

I throw my hands up. "All right, because you have to know,

I'm not sure if I should marry Louis, and I need some good hard time to process that."

Mason is busy dumping LEGOs onto the carpet and then tossing them around, so they make a clanking sound that he giggles at. Mum swivels her head back his way, making sure he's okay, and then walks to where I stand at the counter.

"I knew your father wasn't the one when I married him," she says bluntly.

It's the last thing in the world I expected to come from her mouth, and my jaw drops in shock. "Wha ... What?"

She shrugs, as if I've asked for this explanation of her pre-marriage psyche for nothing more than a good story.

"When we first started dating, it was that honeymoon stage of being in a new relationship. We overlooked the underlying flaws because it was lustful and exciting. In those days, when you were with a person for the amount of time we'd been dating, you took the next logical step. He proposed, and I accepted because it was what I was supposed to do. I planned a wedding, just like a proper woman is expected to. I went along with the charade of committed love because I had paired off, and wasn't that a relief in this harsh world we're born into? But I knew, deep down. In the months leading up to the wedding, I knew in my heart that it wasn't right. That although your father was a good man, one who would care for me and do right by me, I wasn't in love with him. It felt safer, easier to become his wife. But he wasn't *the one*. Sometimes I curse myself for not holding out for whoever the universe had planned for me. Perhaps I missed him when I decided to walk down the aisle to your father. The moment the priest declared us husband and wife, I remember thinking, 'Is this it?' I would never want you to feel that way, Lara."

Leave it to Mum not to lend advice, but tell some sage story about the lesson she was really trying to impart on you. I wish she'd just come out definitively and tell me what to do, but that's a coward's way out on my part and we both know it.

"It's him, though, isn't it? Mason's father?" Mum asks the question we both know the answer to.

I nod because there is nothing else to say.

14

VANCE

"Mate, you're coming up to London soon?" Kingston asks as we perform the ultimate male hug of coming close and clapping each other on the back but not quite being sappy or emotional at all. It was like blokes could hug, but it still had to have a manly air about it.

"I'll be there for the match against Loyale. We don't have an academy match that weekend, and I'll be back from leave," I assure him.

"Who knows, maybe Niles will call you up as a backup for Remus." Jude tries to raise my spirits.

My eyes must convey the sarcasm jumping into my voice. "Right, and pigs are going to fly, as well."

We're standing in the driveway of my parent's home, their bags already stowed in Jude's boot. It's been a great two days with them, even if most of it I spent sulking. They're my best mates, they're used to my funks and moods. After the disaster at the pub, we drove home and drowned in video games for hours. Way too much FIFA, scotch, and ridiculous topics of conversation were had, but it reminded me of our academy days and that brought a certain comfort to my soul.

For a very long time, it had been the three of us. We'd done nothing and everything, but Jude and Kingston had been such a constant in my life that I miss those days now that they're gone. We're in different places, both location wise and in a life sense. They both have weddings to plan and women to keep happy. Jude has his clothing line, and Kingston is busy supporting Poppy in her nonprofit work. I still keep in touch, but it's getting more difficult.

Especially with the circus that is my life.

I can't believe I kissed Lara. I hadn't meant to do it, truly. I'm aware how it cocks everything up, even more than it already is. And now, she's livid. She stormed out of that pub, her friend following her wide-eyed. I could barely get her to respond to me, and I only have five days left.

My bloody cock and his fucking urges. Yes, I am blaming this on him.

"She'll come around, Vance." Jude rouses me from my thoughts.

I must have zoned out. "I'm not sure about that. Pigs may need to fly on that account, too."

"Remember how much I cocked up with Poppy? And she still wants to marry me," Kingston points out.

"I was in the same boat with Aria, too." Jude nods in agreement.

My hands motion for them to see reason. "Mates, you're my closest friends, but don't pretend this is anything like those situations. If I don't play this right, I lose my child."

They exchange a solemn look, and Jude claps me on the shoulder. "It will all work out. It has too. You're Vance Morley, you're the best of us. If the universe allowed us to get our birds, there is no way it's going to deny you a happy ending."

I hug them both one more time, just because I can without feeling like a sap, and then they get in Jude's car and drive away.

And I'm left in Brighton, alone in my head once more.

Wandering back into the house, I figure I'll rustle up some lunch and then really put a plan in motion for approaching Lara again. The clock is ticking, and my luck is about to run out. I texted her yesterday asking if she and Mason would like to come by the house, but she hasn't responded.

My parent's home is all glass and steel, a modern rock overlooking the sea. It's not what I would have chosen, but when they were touring houses, my Mum got set on it and I wasn't going to say no. They deserved this, and I wasn't the one who had to live here full time.

"Are those daft goons gone?" Harlow says as I walk into the kitchen.

I chuckle. "Yes, they're gone. Tired of the noise?"

My sister shakes her head. "I swear, Kingston's favorite sound in the world is his own voice. I don't know how Poppy puts up with him."

"Love is a mysterious thing. Hey, can you make me a sandwich?" I'm used to people waiting on me.

Being home has been freeing in a sense, but losing the component of my life where everything is just at my fingertips is a weird change.

"Bugger off!" She snorts.

"It was worth a try." I begin pulling items out of the refrigerator to make myself lunch.

"So, what are you planning on doing for the rest of your leave?" Harlow asks.

Just in case Lara does accept my invitation for Mason to come play at the house, I'm going to need her to make herself scarce. But if she has to know, which I won't divulge, my mission for the rest of the week is to insert myself in my son's life.

"Some things here, some things there. When do you go back to uni?"

It has to be soon, maybe even before my Mum and Dad get back. They had a holiday scheduled before Harlow and I decided to come home, and we both told them not to cancel it. It worked in my favor, since I'll be able to give Lara and Mason some privacy in our home while also discussing next steps.

I just hope she shows tomorrow.

"Day after next. It was a splendid break home, though."

"When Mum and Dad get home, will you let me know? I have something I need to speak with them about."

Maybe I could schedule her a massage at the spa down by the pier ...

"What, that you have a son they don't know about?"

I almost choke on my own lungs, that's how much Harlow stuns me in the moment. I have to bend over, clapping myself on the chest as I struggle to breathe.

"What did you just say?" I think I may need to clean my ears out.

Harlow spoons a bit of yogurt into her mouth, as if we're talking about the weather, and shrugs. "I didn't realize we were still pretending that Lara Logan's son isn't yours, too. That is why you're in town, isn't it?"

I can't even come up with a coherent thought. "Wha ..."

"Get a grip, Vance. Anyone in this town who doesn't realize you're that boy's father is a daft, blind git. I knew it the first time I saw him, he's the spitting image of you."

"Why ... Why didn't you ever say anything?" I sputter, still trying to regain my composure.

She leans against the counter and shrugs. "I guess because I thought you'd come to me when you wanted to discuss it."

"I didn't know." My voice grows quiet.

"What?" Now it's Harlow's turn to sound blindsided. "What do you mean, you didn't know?"

"She never told me. I only saw him just mere weeks ago,

when I was home on holiday. I had no idea he even existed until recently. Or else ... yes, I suppose I would have come to you."

Harlow sets down her yogurt, her empty hands flexing and opening as if she can't help it.

"And here, I didn't like the girl when you were sneaking around with her to begin with. I'm going to give her a piece of my mind, that—"

My hand comes up in a harsh motion. "Don't finish that sentence. There is a lot you don't know. Apparently, though, my time with Lara isn't one of them. How did you know?"

"Vance, I'm a woman. One who lived in your house when you were around and can see past this rhino hide you wear like skin. I'm not an idiot, but everyone else seems to be. You were madly in love with that girl from the day her family moved in across the street."

I shrug, because she's right. "Yes, that sums it up. Everything that's happened from that point though, it's a disaster."

"He looks exactly like you," Harlow murmurs.

How no one has guessed that Mason is my son before my sister is actually rather incredible. He is my carbon copy, and in this town, it's not a secret what I look like. Even as a bloke who grew up here, I still get people asking me for autographs on the street.

"I know he does. It ... it's killing me inside not to see him every day. Since the moment I saw him, I've just ... there is this inexplicable yearning to be close to him. To wake him up every morning and put him down to bed every night. Is that mental? I didn't know three months ago that I was a father, and now that I do, I want to be the best parent anyone has ever been."

"Well, you're an overachiever with a perfectionist complex, so that's not surprising. But no, it's not mental. I've wanted to go up to her so many times when I see them in town, but I didn't know if you had an agreement. Mum and Dad don't even know they have a grandson."

My head falls into my hands, and I rake them through my hair. "I know that, too. It's why I'm going to tell them when they get home. At least I don't have to tell you, too."

"What are you going to do, Vance?" She says it so quietly, as if it isn't the questioning I've been asking myself since the moment I walked out of that wine shop.

My answer has always been the same in terms of going after things I want.

"Whatever I have to."

15

LARA

When I pull into the driveway of the house Mason's parents now live in, my jaw almost drops to the floor of my previously owned, but decently tidy, average car.

This was a long way from Willingham Street, the neighborhood Vance and I had grown up in.

Don't get me wrong, Brighton is a wonderful place to grow up as a child. Neither of our families was below the poverty line, we had new clothes each school year and presents under the Christmas tree.

But this brand of financial wealth? No, this is not the way the Morley's used to live.

I've never actually driven through their neighborhood, though I live fifteen minutes from it; some irrational paranoia inside me assumed they'd be standing at the end of the driveway if I ever tried, ready to snatch my son away.

The home is gated at the front, as if the Queen lives here, and once I ring a bell at the entrance, they swing open to reveal the reflective enormity of his parent's place. The sides of the home are sharp angles of glass, no brick or shingles here. It looks like one of those modern majesties you see in a design magazine, as if an artist had constructed it. It's not my taste, but it is beautiful in its own way.

"Look who's here!"

Vance has put on his "talking to a child voice," and it's kind of melting my ovaries. He walks out to my car, where I've parked in the driveway, and opens the back door.

Mason makes a gleeful sound, and before I can instruct Vance on how to get him out of the car seat, he's pulling the little boy from the back and into his arms.

"I hear you want to go find fish in the ocean."

"It's twenty degrees, Vance," I scold him, pulling Mason's nappy bag from the car.

"We can put our coats on. Come on, Mummy," he goads Mason, completely ignoring the fact that we had a blow-up at each other just days ago.

"Come on, Mummy!" Mason echoes his biological father.

The two of them, standing there in cahoots, makes me break. A smile involuntarily graces my lips, and I roll my eyes.

"Fine, but only if you wear mittens and a cap, too." I sigh, relenting.

They dash into the house, and I'm left to walk in by myself, gasping at the ridiculous amount of rooms and lush furnishing in his parent's house. When he asked me to come today, I honestly didn't know if I'd bring Mason. I thought about coming alone, reprimanding him for kissing me and setting down strict guidelines. But then Vance asked for some pictures of Mason to save on his phone, and I realized what an arse I was being. He just wants to see his son, and the one thing I've kept from him for so long ... it's the least I could give him.

Watching his face light up as Mason's little voice prattles on and on about his childhood nonsense, there is nothing like it. I used to get joy out of watching Louis with my son, but it was a muted glee. Because deep down, I knew he wasn't his father.

Watching Vance interact with the little boy we brought into the world is every fantasy I've dreamed come to life.

I drove around Brighton yesterday afternoon after I left Mason at Mum's. To no one's surprise, least of all my own, I ended up on the beach. The one Vance had found me on all those Christmas's ago.

I sat there, staring at the sea, willing it to give me an answer. Should I stay with him, should I go? Do I tell him about the kiss, or scrub it from my own memory? How do I handle Vance wanting to come into our son's life, into my life?

So many questions, tough, unthinkable, vitally important questions. If I only had to answer one of them, maybe I'd be more equipped to do so. But, I've created this mountain, one that was once a molehill. I could have come clean with Louis right away, with all of them. I could have not kept the mystery of Mason's biological father from the people closest to me. I could have told Vance he had a child and dealt with it from the start.

Instead, I created the nightmare I am living in. It's not as if Vance is the only guilty party in that kiss. Bloody hell, it's burned into my brain, how spectacular that fleeting moment had been. To feel his lips on mine again, to experience the pure magic of our connection ...

I didn't realize how long I've been waiting to have that again. Now that I have, I'm not sure I can go back to a life starved of it.

If Mum had told me to stay with Louis, instead of feeding me her wise metaphorical story, I probably wouldn't even be here. I would have put this out of my brain, told Vance I couldn't do this and somehow convince him to leave us in our sheltered, but content bubble. But she didn't. So now, I stand in his family's home, watching as he pretends to make elephant noises for our son, and I know my heart will never be the same.

Mum has never pressed the issue of Mason's parentage. Perhaps because the first and only two times she tried to tackle the subject, I snapped at her. The first was when I had just revealed my pregnancy to her, and she sobbed and asked who had done it to me. It was the most irrational and emotional I've ever seen her.

The second, and final, time she asked was when Mason was about a month old, and he so vividly resembled Vance it hurt me to look at him some days. Something inside me thinks she knows who his father is, since my son is the picture of the boy across the street.

Maybe she knows, and would rather me follow the thorny, dangerous path. The one filled with obstacles and no promises. But if I could make it to the end of the tightrope walk, I would be blissfully, unequivocally happy.

Maybe she regrets that she didn't take that route.

After a few minutes of rough-housing and toddler babbling inside, both boys insist we go out to the private beach behind the house. With its soaring views and private ocean-side serenity, it's no wonder Vance's parents picked this home.

"Don't you splash me!" Vance teases Mason, flicking tiny dots of seafoam at him as they balance on the rocks.

"Splash! Bubbles!" Mason shrieks, his little nose red.

He's so happy, I don't have the heart to be mean Mum and enforce the rules before he catches cold.

"Run! Fast!" Mason races around the shore, taunting at the water.

Vance has to double over at one point he's laughing so hard, because Mason keeps sticking his fingers in the water and then his faces screws up from the salt he's licking off his hands.

I'm participating, but more as a referee for possibly dangerous situations. That's my job as a mum, to keep my child from harm. I'm just not sure yet if his real father wanting to be in his life is one of those.

Around mid-afternoon, I see the telltales signs of exhaustion in Mason's eyes.

"He should have a nap," I tell Vance as he removes my son's socks and shoes.

Mason is sipping a small amount of hot chocolate from a mug, with Vance's help, and I'm amazed by how well he can multitask with the toddler. He's a natural parent, and I'm not sure why I thought he wouldn't be.

"There is a guest room on this floor."

My heart is a puddle in my chest cavity watching Vance carry Mason. My son's head is tucked into his father's neck, their dark hair meshing. I want to mold into that embrace, to be one unit, together with them.

Does Mason know who this man is? He's usually friendly toward those he hasn't met, he's not a shy child, but the way he connects with Vance is different. He barely knows him and you can see the twinkle of recognition between them.

When Vance signals to the door where my boy can nap, he transfers Mason to my arms and I take him inside. It only takes a few minutes of rocking and humming before his eyes droop closed, and I tiptoe out quietly.

"He's sleeping." I come out of the room, careful not to shut the door in case Mason wakes up in search of me.

"Easily knackered, yeah?" Vance smiles, peaking through the open crack at our snoozing boy.

He stands there for a while, a gentle giant watching his son sleep peacefully. I realize that he has never had the pleasure of watching Mason drift off into a dream state, of watching this tiny human we created soothe himself to sleep.

"It's wonderful, isn't it?" I nudge in next to him, admiring my son.

"What's that?" Vance doesn't turn to look at me but keeps his eyes trained on Mason.

"Watching him dream. I often wonder what's going on in that precious brain." Smiling slightly, I pull Vance away by the elbow. "Let him nap."

He follows reluctantly. "I never get to see him do that."

One of those pangs of guilt, the ones becoming too frequent, pinches at my heart as Vance and I make our way out to the living room.

"I know. We should talk about that."

Vance is quiet, shocker. He blinks twice, waiting for me to go on.

"I want you to be in his life. It's clear you want to care for him, to be around him and help nurture him. I can't deny you, or him, that any longer. It's not going to be easy, there are many people who will not like the idea of this. And I also don't want Mason paraded to the press because of who you are. So, while it will be an adjustment for our families, I do not want to keep you from knowing our son."

I thought long and hard about this. Yesterday, in my alone time, I put my feelings aside and looked at it objectively. The man who helped create my child wants to love him and be a part of his life. Vance has never been cruel, always been responsible, has a stable job and his head on straight. Why should I turn away a person in this world who wishes to care for Mason?

"He is too important to me to ever let anything get out to the tabloids. I have people for that. It will be handled," he assures me.

"Thank you. And ... I'm sorry, Vance. I never meant for this to spin so out of control. I should have told you from the start. I'm sincerely sorry that I was so daft."

A beat passes, and my cheeks redden. Is he just going to stand there and stare at me?

"And what about us?" Vance asks, apparently not satisfied with all I just compromised.

As if my apology means shite to him.

"I'm engaged, Vance. To marry another man. Stop this." My voice is stone cold.

"You kissed me. That means something." He pushes at the wound, scraping it with his fingernail.

I can feel my blood heat. "That was a mistake. One I'll be locking in a vault and never thinking about again. I want you to be in my son's life, your son's life, and that's all this is."

"If that's what you need to keep telling yourself." His voice is almost smug.

The hairpin in the grenade that is my temper dislodges.

"To the rest of the world, you're the good bloke. Their mate, their reliable, dependable guy. You like to see yourself in that lens, when the one I see you through is that of the man who walked out and never looked back. You chose to leave, Vance. For the first time in your life, you didn't stick it out. You quit, bloody gave up on us because it was hard! To me, you're not the anchor you pride yourself on being. You're my hurricane, the storm that blows through and decimates my entire landscape. You cast me as the villain, the bird who didn't tell you about your son. But to me, you're to blame. You abandoned me long before I decided to get even. Neither of us is right, but stop making me the evil one here."

I can barely breathe by the time I come up for air, adrenaline singeing my veins.

Vance stares me down, both of us two wrongs that I'm not sure will ever be able to make this right.

He's winded, his chest heaving with each intake of air, and the crackle of *us* snaps in the air.

"Can I kiss you? Again?"

At least he asked this time. It's inevitable, this thing between us. Even if we're burning the world around us to ashes, we'll always come back to it.

I know better and should say no. In my bones, though, I know I won't. I'm a hypocrite, an utter fool. Two seconds ago, I was insisting that we mean nothing to each other outside the realm of our child, and now I am all but pressed up against him.

I can only nod my consent, too much of a coward to agree out loud, and then he's on me.

16

LARA

His hands thread through my hair, our bodies meeting in the most glorious of ways as Vance pushes me against the wall.

The weight of him, the musky, rugged scent of those large limbs, it consumes me. My mouth latches to his, the friction of our lips causing a spark. Neither of us jump back, we ride through the moment of pain, our lips digging into the others even deeper.

Our tongues meet, doing the hedonistic dance that feels so much naughtier than snogging. From the first moment he kissed me, on the shores of our hometown, there has been something electric between us. I've never felt it with anyone else, not the boys I kissed or allowed to feel under my pushup bra when I was a teenager.

Not even Louis.

The sheer energy between Vance and I is a once in a lifetime kind of chemistry. One that I've missed every single day we've been apart, even if I have promised myself to another man.

Vance is vicious as he uses his mouth on mine and his hands on my neck to coax moans from deep within my body. Every cell buzzes with excitement, and I can't help but grind my hips against his. The rigid length of him presses right back, and I know intimately just how large that hidden steel is. The hairs on the back of my neck stand up on end thinking about Vance laying me down on a bed.

I can't help myself, I sneak a hand under his long-sleeve thermal, my fingertips connecting with scorching, rock-hard abs. The feel of his bare skin has my head spinning, and my knees buckle.

We're alone in this house, our son is sound asleep in the next room and there is no one in sight. This isn't a pub hallway, there are no spectators around. If I want this to happen, for him to take me into his bedroom and remind me of how spectacular we are together, there is no more dangerous place than right here. I'm vulnerable, all alone with him. My walls are down, my sensibilities out the window.

"Take it off," Vance growls, edging his fingers under the hem of my sweater.

All at once, reality slams back into me, just like it did in the pub. What am I *doing*? This is wrong, so bloody wrong.

"Stop, *stop*!" I push him back, and our hands dislodge from under each other's shirts. "Bloody hell ... *fuck*."

What the hell am I doing? My mind races, tears pricking at the backs of my eyes.

"Lara, don't you feel this?" Vance grabs at his shirt, fisting the material as if he's trying to clutch his heart. "You can't tell me this is how it feels with him. I bloody love you, every inch of you!"

My lungs seize, contracting at a rapid rate. It feels like I might be having a panic attack, every motion of my limbs fraught with severe anxiety and fear of everything I just did, and what it might mean for all that I've built.

I can't believe I just did that. I can't believe I cheated on

Louis, for the second time. That I went against the promise I made him, that I'm threatening the good thing we have going.

It's telling, in a way, that Louis is my second thought. Because my first ones? They're all about Vance.

How incredible his lips felt on mine. How out of control but powerful being intimate with him makes me feel. How intense our connection is. How I never want to stop experiencing that.

How I could do it for the rest of my life.

"You're only saying this now because I'm off-limits, Vance. Because you can't have unfettered access to me, like you used to. All those years ago, do you remember how much you led me on? I was in a permanent tizzy because of your hot and cold personality. You only want me now because the chase is forbidden."

"I've wanted you since the day I laid eyes on you when I was ten. I've wanted you always because when I see you, I can barely breathe. The only reason I left you was because we were doing more harm than good to each other."

"As if that's not what we're doing now?" I counter, my voice reed thin.

"Only because you're resisting it. I never stopped wanting you, that was never the problem. Blimey, I've thought about you more in the last two years than I thought about my career. And you know me, deeply know me, so you know that's saying something. Don't marry him, Lara. I'll be the chump, the bastard who asks you to act solely for his selfish gains. Because if you don't, we'll both be miserable the rest of our lives."

Now, I start to cry, really letting the tears that I've kept at bay flow down over my cheeks. They feel good, a release in a sense when I'm forced to hold everything else inside.

"You blew back into town like some kind of hurricane on a mission. Like those awful storms that wreck the shoreline and damage entire houses. You toppled mine. It only took you less than two weeks to dismantle my universe."

"It must have not been a very stable universe."

The sentence itself seems arrogant, but Vance does not deliver it in a cocky manner. It's more melancholy, as if he's sad for me. Sad for what he is doing, but not sorry for it.

"I don't even know which way is up," I say this more to myself than I say it to him, raking my hands through my hair.

Vance turns his back to me, and I feel the restless upset rolling off of him.

"I'm here for five more days. You have a lot of decisions to make, Lara. I can't make them for you, and you already know my answer on each one. I just ... I hope you know that if you choose *us*, you and me, I will never let you down again."

Out of all the things he could say, any way he could campaign for himself, that simple message is not what I was expecting.

But Vance is a man of his word, and it stings to know it could only be that easy for him.

For me, this is going to be the toughest five days of my life ... and I have been through a lot of shite in my past, so *that's* saying something.

17

LARA

Two days of school pass and I barely notice with all the things I have rattling around in my brain.

I go through the motions, grading papers, teaching classes, dealing with student's problems, and attending meetings with my coworkers. Stef and I eat lunch together, and I listen as she gripes about her noisy neighbor and the awful date she went on over the weekend.

After school, it's all eyes on Mason, and I focus all of my energy on showing him all the love I can.

And then he goes to sleep, and I'm stuck in the prison I've constructed for myself. The one where I go over and over all the decisions in my head and try to keep a smile on my face in front of Louis. The one where I know the right thing I must do, but lie down in bed next to a man that I have not been faithful to.

Stef walks into my classroom at the end of the day, her hands on her hips as if she means business. "It's been days, and I have not come in here with my temper and demanded answers. Be proud of me."

I snort. "Then why does it look like you're about to do just that?"

She sighs heavily, collapsing into one of the front desks in my classroom. "Perhaps I am. You know you can't leave me in this perpetual state of guessing. It's not good for my heart. I'm just not strong enough."

Rolling my eyes, I set down the red marker I was using to grade essays. "As if your life is being affected by my personal business."

"When it has to do with the three hottest footballers in all of England, *yes*, it is affecting me." She points a hot pink fingernail at me.

Count on Stef to paint her nails neon as winter touches down.

"What do you want to know?" I sigh.

If she's going to force me to talk about it, she can be the one to ask for the information she wants. I'm too mentally exhausted to go through the entire history of Vance and me.

Her eyes narrow. "You're an arse. Making me do all the work. Fine. How do you know those guys?"

"I don't really. Not anymore. But Vance Morley grew up in Brighton, so you could say I know them through him."

"I forgot he grew up here. That, Stef pauses, makes a little more sense. But, it doesn't sound like you knew Jude Davies or Kingston Phillips." It's like she's trying to piece together a puzzle.

I'm too stubborn to just put them all together for her. "I didn't."

Stef shoots daggers at me. "You're not making this easy. Why was Vance Morley eye-shagging you the entire time?"

That makes me almost choke on my own breath. "He wasn't. Trust me."

Actually, he probably was. I just can't handle thinking about that right now. In my head, I'm trying to decide whether or not to call off an engagement to a man who has only been kind and supportive to me. Thinking about shagging Vance will only confuse me more than I already am.

"Um, yes, he was. I was afraid that giant Adonis was going to launch himself across the table and try to put his knob in you with all of us still sitting there."

Blimey, talk about *not* trying to think about Vance naked and randy. Thanks for nothing, Stef.

"He's Mason's father," I blurt out, and then slap a hand over my mouth the moment I realize what I've done.

Well, that escalated quickly.

I've not even told my own mother that vital fact, and here I am, telling Stef with my classroom door wide open. Not that I'm fearful of what she might do with the information, she's the closest friend I have. She would never do anything to jeopardize Mason or me in any way.

It's just shocking that I actually came clean about my son's father, almost without even thinking about doing so.

"I had a feeling." Her eyes hold mine in a significant look.

I think she knows how hard it was for me to confess that. Or maybe she realizes how difficult it's been to keep it hidden.

"You can't tell anyone that," I whisper through the fingers covering my lips.

Stef rises from the desk, walks to where I sit and covers my hand with hers. "You know I would never do that. Was that why he came looking for you? Why *were* his goons with him?"

I shrug, but I think I know why after all the reflection I've been doing. "It's a very long story, one I don't have time or enough alcohol in my system for right now. But, Vance and I were together a long time ago, and he never let me meet them. I think this was some kind of olive branch."

"What happened between you two near the toilets? You ran out of that pub and to your car like you'd been slapped. Wait, he didn't put hands on you, did he? That *hijo de puta*, I'll kick him into next month."

A chuckle comes from my lips, because I would like to see that. But then my mood sombers.

"No. Well ... he did, in an all too good way. Not good in our situation, but—"

"You two kissed, didn't you?" Stef puts me out of the misery of trying to explain my adultery.

I nod, confirming the worst of it. "I didn't mean for it to happen. I would—I've never been that person. I would never do that to Louis. But ... I did."

My voice is tinged with tears, with pain, and Stef gets up to close the door.

"What are you going to do?" she asks, her voice close, though I can't see her with my head buried in my hands.

"I can't figure it out. I do like my life, what I have with Louis, our bond with Mason. But—"

"It's always the *but* that gets you. I know I'm not objective, we both know how I feel about your fiancé. But, I have to say, Lara, if you're even inviting that doubt into the life you claim you like—and you said like, not love—I think you have your answer."

My head raises to meet her gaze. "How am I supposed to do that to Louis?"

"Would you be able to go into a life, a marriage, with him knowing that you have absolutely no feelings for the father of your child?"

I want to break down in sobs because no, I cannot. I wish I could rid my brain of any memory of Vance Morley. To forget that I kissed him not once, but twice, while wearing another man's ring.

So I just shake my head.

Stef holds my hand again, squeezing because she knows how tough the next stage in my life will be.

"Then, again, I say, you have your answer."

Walking into my flat, that death march music plays in blaring, obnoxious swells in my brain.

With every step, I feel the weight on my shoulders come down heavier, the tears in my chest drowning my heart. I don't want to go in there, don't want to have to face the terrible decisions I've made.

In talking with Stef, though, in seeing just how plain and simple the answers are, I know I have to do this.

I have to walk into the flat we share, and tell Louis, my fiancé, that I'm not going to marry him.

And that explanation has to come with owning up to the worst truth of them all; that I cheated on him. That I kissed another man, twice, knowing full well what I was doing. I can blame lust and my history with Vance blinding me, but I was aware of the disaster I was creating. Blimey, the second time, I gave him permission.

This is it, I think as my hand rests on the knob to our front door. I'm about to destroy everything I hold sacred behind this door.

If I'm being honest, I already did that the first time I let Vance Morley crowd my space. When I admitted, silently to myself, that I still love him, too.

I push my key into the door and enter my flat, feeling guilty that I waited until Mason was in bed but also knowing I couldn't do this with my child in the room. I could have waited, sat Louis down later, but the moment I knew I was going to break this off, there was no way I could keep it off my face when he saw me.

"Hey, love, glad you're home. Little bugger went down after three books, but I've got wine poured so we can both relax."

My average, wonderful, compassionate fiancé walks into the room holding the stems, dark red wine jiggling in the bulbs atop them.

"I cheated on you." The words drop like anvils on my heart.

Louis's head tilts slowly, his eyes blinking and the smile that just graced his lips slides right off.

"What?" His voice is all kinds of cautious, as if he expects me to tell him I'm just joking.

As if, in just a second, I'll double over with laughter and yell, "Got ya!"

But I can't do that. Because it isn't true.

"I cheated. I kissed someone else. Twice."

I hadn't known if I was going to lead with this. If I could just walk in here and sit him down, explain that I couldn't go through with our wedding or marriage because of my own feelings. Part of me wanted to spare him the pain of my traitorous actions. But, in the end, I knew it wouldn't be fair. He needed the entire story, to know the damage I'd done.

And in a way, I needed to admit to it. Because carrying that secret around with me for just a few days was eating me alive. I still felt like shite, but at least it wasn't devouring me from the inside.

Calmly, so calmly that I think he might fly off the handle after he cracks, Louis puts the wineglasses down. He stands up straight, pinches the bridge of his nose, and then nods his head.

"Okay. Okay. Who?" His voice is hurt, but almost hopeful, as if he's looking for a way through this.

Oh, Louis. Sweet, kind Louis. He's going to try to fix this.

So, I have to be the one to ruin it. For both of us. I do not want to marry him, and he shouldn't have to live with my behavior for the rest of his life. We're not a match, and I have to show him that.

"With Mason's father."

Now, he blows out a breath, an angry huff that guts me. "Jesus fucking Christ. Really, Lara? The guy who hasn't been here one bloody day of Mason's life? That's who you fell into the gutter with? Bloody ... *fuck!*"

The volume of his words ticks up a couple of notches, and I want to tell him to quiet down because of the boy sleeping in the next room, but I fear it will only make this worse.

"I didn't mean for it to happen ..." I try to explain.

"When? When did he get into town? Or has he always been here? Christ, I'm never even allowed to bring him up, so how would I know? Has he been smirking at me across the downtown streets for years, laughing at the man trying to marry the woman who actually loves him instead?"

"No, never, I would never do that to you—" Reason and rational speech evade me.

This isn't what I thought it would be. I'm not sure what I was expecting, who can when they break up with someone, but Louis has always been the level-headed one. He's the one who calms me down, who talks in a quiet voice when Mason is upset. I realize now that he won't be that for us anymore, that he isn't even on our team from this point on. We're opponents, and he has no loyalty to reason with me anymore.

"No, you'd just cheat on me with the bloke who up and left you as a pregnant teenager," he spits, and I realize also that I've never seen the nasty side of Louis.

Snot and tears clog my throat, choke me and blind me, so I reach out to touch his hands. "I'm so sorry, Louis. I-I never meant for this—"

He tears his hands away, and I feel the heartbreak rolling off of him in waves. "It's always been him, hasn't it?"

I want to smack myself. Or possibly perform a lobotomy to

forget Vance Morley ever existed. That would solve all of this, and it would present Louis as the only option; I could love him without hesitation.

But would I? Even if I never met Vance, wouldn't it feel as if there was a love greater than the one I had, just waiting for me to discover it? Just like Mum said she wished she'd waited? I suppose it would. And since I discovered that love *before* Louis, it ... has always been Vance.

"Yes," I whisper, horrifying myself.

Louis shakes his head. "I ... I don't even know what to say. I'm livid, at you. I'm livid at myself."

Tears spill from my eyes. "This is my fault. Blame me, I did this."

"Oh, believe me, I do. I've given you all of me, I've taken care of your child as if he's my own. We've built this life together, and I thought if I nudged us along, you'd catch up. Apparently, I am a bloody idiot. But, an idiot who knew better. I've seen it on your face for years, that you'd never love me like you love him."

Throwing Mason in my face is low, but I deserve it. Part of me wants to fire back, to know if he ever really loved Mason like his own. But I know better. I welcome the insults and shame; I deserve them.

"I'm sorry. I truly am." I wipe at my eyes. "You should have this."

With a tug, I remove the ring he gave me from my finger and hold it in my palm for him to take.

"When I gave this to you, I thought we'd be together forever. You did this, Lara. I want you to know when Mason wakes up and I'm not here, when he comes home from school next week and I'm not here, you will have to explain why. When our wedding date rolls around, and you feel that guilt in your heart, know that *you* did this."

Louis snatches the ring from my hand, marches to the door, grabs his keys and coat, and then he's gone.

In less than five minutes, I successfully drove away the only father my son has ever known.

I slump to the floor, sobbing into my hands.

18

VANCE

While Lara sorts her shite out at home, I need to get my house in order.

And the first item on the agenda is telling my parents that they have a grandchild. One who has lived not ten minutes from them for the last year and a half.

Still, as I wait for my parents to arrive home from their holiday in Switzerland, I can't help but wonder what Lara is doing. What is she thinking? Has she called off her wedding, left her fiancé? Is she working through it, choosing to stay with him?

The thought of that almost obliterates my heart.

I know I'm pushing her, that I'm driving her to her limits. I'm being selfish and ornery, demanding and immovable.

But I've never known another way. Something inside me demands precision in the way I live, and apparently, the way I love. If I want it, I won't stop until I achieve it.

And this is the love of my life I'm talking about. The son that I helped bring into this world. If I don't fight tooth and nail for them, if I accept no as an answer when it comes to the most vital people in my life, what good is living?

There aren't enough people in this world who go after what

they want unapologetically. We all tiptoe around each other, careful not to tread on feet or offend. And by doing that, we settle for second best. We settle for unhappiness or sometimes even straight out misery.

I'm not willing to do that.

I'm a bloody git for breaking up with Lara, for holding a torch for two years and never telling her. If I have even an icicles chance in hell to get her back, I'm going after it with all the might and energy I have.

When Mum and Dad walk through the door, weekend satchels in hand from their holiday, Harlow and I will be waiting for them in the sitting room.

It's the most formal room in the house, and also the one closest to the door. In the twenty-four hours since Lara left after bringing Mason to visit, Harlow and I have gone over and over what I'll say to our parents. The past two weeks have contained the most amount of talking I've done in years, and I'm conversationally exhausted. But, I know I can't be done having discussions just yet.

"Stop tapping your foot, you look mental," Harlow chides.

I send her a glare. "Do you know how uncomfortable I am?"

My skin feels too tight, has felt that way since I stepped back into town. While I am a definitive, laser-focused kind of man, expressing my emotions is something I simply care little for. I care so little for it that I'd rather bungee jump off a bridge instead of have a deep talk, and heights make me rather wonky.

"I couldn't tell in the least," Harlow responds sarcastically.

The sound of a key scraping into a lock comes from the front door, and then Mum and Dad are walking through it.

"How was your trip?" My sister jumps off the settee.

I think she's trying to butter them up before I lead them off a cliff they definitely will not want to go over, and I silently thank her for it by sending an appreciative glance her way. She tips her head, almost a *you're welcome*.

"Well, what do we owe this nice welcoming committee to?" Mum beams as she sets her bags down.

"We just wanted to make sure you had a wonderful holiday," Harlow answers.

"It was splendid. We hiked some of the Alps, and I brought home some delicious Swiss coffee," Dad tells us.

I mostly look like my father, a raven-haired man who is now graying at the temple. But still, my old man has that eagle-eyed sharpness about him, the introverted intellect he passed down to me. He's lightened up some since we've gotten older, but he still has his singular interests, physical exercise and good coffee being two of them.

Mum is softer, more outgoing like Harlow, and a natural blond. They met when they were eight, and began dating at the age of sixteen. Brighton born and bred, my parents have never considered living anywhere else. They're good people, with good attitudes and work ethics, who raised their children to be morally appropriate. I've always tried to live up to their standards, which is why this conversation is going to be so difficult.

"Can you come sit with us in the living room?" I ask, trying to sound kind.

I think the effect is more along the lines of the Beast asking Belle to have dinner with him in his ballroom, because my family looks at me like I've nearly lost my head.

"Sure, darling," Mum says, her eyes curious and shocked at the same time.

We move into the parlor, and I take a seat on the sofa across from my parents, who sit on the same one.

I look to Harlow, willing her to talk first. But she stands firm, crossing her arms over her chest where she sits on the arm of my parent's sofa.

"A year and a half ago, Lara Logan had a baby," I begin, trying to wade slowly into this mad house.

Dad nods matter-of-factly. "We know. Your Mum bumped into hers at the market a few times."

"Never seen the little lad, but I bet he's beautiful. Lara always was so pretty," Mum gushes.

"Hmm, I wondered if you'd seen him," Harlow throws in.

We're both thinking the same thing; if my parents had seen Mason, they'd have known instantly that he's a Morley.

"I only met him a few months ago. I ..." I don't know where I should begin, where this story makes sense to begin telling.

"Okay ...?" My mother waves her hand, rolling it at the wrist as if telling me to speed this up.

"I'm rather hungry, Vance," Dad puts in, and I realize they're probably both knackered from the trip.

Best to just come out with it, then. "I am the father of her child. My child. Mason, her son, is ... well, he's my son. I have a son."

I swear, you could hear a bloody pin drop for at least two minutes in the Morley household.

When Mum has sobered enough to pick her jaw up off the floor, she shrieks, "*What!*"

"I didn't even know you two were ... involved," Dad mutters, and with the faraway look glazing over his eyes, I know he's trying to internally piece this all together.

"We dated for about two years, from the time we were seventeen until about nineteen," I supply.

"We still lived in the house across the street! You're telling me you were dating Lara Logan, and no one knew about it?" Mum looks flabbergasted.

I shrug sheepishly. "I've never been one to publicly acknowledge my love life."

"No, you just appear in magazines with a new model every

other week. Vance Morley, I raised you better. You never once brought that girl over for dinner. What does she think of us?" Mum scolds me.

Of course, ignore the fact that I just told you you have a grandchild and begin riding my arse about manners and etiquette.

"You kept this from us?" Dad grunts, as if it's inconceivable.

"I didn't know, Dad. I didn't know he even existed until mere weeks ago."

"How old is he now?" Mum asks another random question.

Their brains must be in overdrive. I know mine was when I found out about Mason.

"He's one and a half. His birthday is in April," I tell them.

"So Lara ... she has hidden him from us? We live in the same town, we lived across the street!" Mum has become incensed. "I have a grandson, that I never knew about? I ... I don't—"

Andddd now she's crying. Openly sobbing, and slumps over onto Dad's shoulder so hard that he has to bring his arms around her body to calm her.

"Oh, Mum." Harlow comes around the other side to comfort her, and tries shushing our mother into just semi-dramatic crying.

I sit on my sofa across the coffee table, feeling like an arsehole. If I hadn't been a prick to Lara, if I'd gotten over my need to segment every part of my life, then maybe we would have stayed together. Maybe I would have known the moment she did that we were pregnant. I could have let my parents know their grandson from the moment he entered the world.

None of that happened, and now, here we are.

"Can we meet him?" Dad suddenly looks up, as if this thought just occurred to him.

And another wave of guilt crashes over me, because I can't promise them that. "Lara and I are still working everything out. I want so much for you to meet him, he's incredible. It ... it's just going to take some time."

Way to be the worst son in the world, mate. Harlow glares at me because I probably could have sugarcoated that a bit more for their sake, but it's just never been my strong suit. White lying, omitting to spare someone's feelings, I never understood that.

"I'll just have to call her mother," Mum says, sitting up straight and wiping her tears in a self-righteous motion.

"Oh, no, Mum, please you don't have to—"

She cuts me off. "There is a little boy running around with our genes, in the same town as us. Of course, I need to see him."

I just brought a storm of hellfire down on my head, and I'd only been meaning to comfort and soothe.

This is exactly why I never talk things out.

19

LARA

The day following Louis's departure, it rains cats and dogs.

Driving, windy sheets of icy rain smash against every building, piece of pavement, roadway, and, seemingly, my heart.

Just because I decided to end things, to be the one to call it off, doesn't mean I'm not devastated. I spent the last two and a half years with the man, formed a strong partnership and a compatible kind of love. Louis was my friend, confidant, and comfort through many a hard time. He was a father to Mason, and half of the household income.

This breakup, it isn't just a boyfriend leaving. It isn't an ill-fitting partner exiting a relationship, or a bastard getting his due finally. No, the end of our relationship is much more like a divorce. We shared tangible, important things, there will need to be a dividing of assets.

And the most damaging part of the split, emotionally, is going to be separating the me I was with Louis, from who I am now. Extracting him from my heart will gut me, because I did it to myself but I also know how much I still care for him.

The doorbell rings, pulling me out of my self-pity.

"Daddy!" Mason jumps up from the floor, where every toy he owns is strewn about the carpet.

I want so desperately for it to be Louis standing on the other side of that door, for my son's sake, but I know that, most likely, it's not. Louis texted me a couple of hours after he stormed out, telling me that he was traveling back home to Wales for a while and would be in touch when he had some space.

So far, Mason has asked no more than three dozen times when his daddy would be back, in that stilted speaking of his.

"I don't think so, buddy." I try not to shed a tear when I say it.

My decision, all of my decisions, no longer effect just me. Louis leaving, of my doing, will damage Mason, too.

I walk to the door, pull it open, and my heart expires in my chest at the sight I see.

A hulking, devastatingly gorgeous Vance Morley. With every piece of clothing he wears wet and plastered to him.

It appears as if the rain has swallowed him whole, his long sleeve and jeans soaked and sticking to every dip and curve of his carved body. My mouth goes dry just looking at him, and it's a losing battle to keep my knickers from becoming as wet as the shock of black hair curling down onto his forehead. His hands brace the sides of my doorway just like they used to brace the sides of my head when he'd move over me in bed. Drips of rain water splash from his long black eyelashes down onto his cheeks, and I want to step toward him and swipe my tongue along the moisture on his bottom lip.

Everything in me vibrates with need and desire, and for a moment, I forget about all the chaos between us. I want him to attack me, to hoist me up onto his hips and barrel through my flat, water splashing everywhere. I want Vance to tumble into my bed and make loud, passionate love to me while our bones chill from the temperature of his clothes and skin.

I'm hot and cold, the affect sending my head spinning.

"Is he gone?" Vance asks, his rough tone like knuckles scraping over the nub of intensity between my legs.

Rain pelts at his back, but he doesn't move inside. "Yes. I-I broke it off last night."

Why I feel like this is some explanation I owe him, or that I should show him what a good girl I am that I called off my engagement for him, I have no clue. He's the one who came to town and upended my life. Yet, with him standing there like that, it feels like I should be the one to beg.

Without being invited, Vance steps inside, puddles of water forming on the floor of my tiny entryway. I don't speak, and he doesn't follow when I retrieve a towel from the linen closet across my flat.

Mason is still unaware of his real father's presence, and I need to keep it that way until Vance and I can talk.

"Thanks," he says as he dabs himself off, and I'm not sure if he means for the towel or for leaving my fiancé.

"I didn't do it for you." That's only half true.

Dark brown eyes, the color of coffee mixed with whiskey, skate over my entire body. As if we're not having a serious conversation, as if this is all some cat and mouse game that will end in him capturing me.

"You might not have left him for me, but don't lie. You did it because you weren't in love with him. Not like you're in love with me."

The selfish bastard. He's so bloody calm and collected all the time that I forget how much of an ego lies dormant under the cool facade. Vance may be the silent one among his merry band of scoundrels, but he's still a scoundrel through and through.

"This isn't some contest you just won, Vance," I spit, my ire evident in my tone.

His dark eyes flash, a streak of lightning at midnight. "You're not with him anymore. It kind of does. I want you, Lara. You're what I've been fighting for. Now, we can have what we desire."

Annoyance flicks at the muscles of my heart because he's being disrespectful.

"You'll excuse me if I'm not just upset about the breakup of my engagement. Because I'm not, I'm devastated. Partially because Louis is a wonderful man who loved me, and I loved him in my own way. Partially because ending a commitment of that caliber is damaging to the soul. I made the man a promise, and he was counting on creating a life with me. But mostly, I'm terribly heartbroken for Mason. Louis is the only father he's ever known, and a man who was a brilliant role model for my son. So, forgive me for not wanting to fall into your arms and weep of romantic elation. I'm horribly sad, Vance. It is going to take some time for me to heal, to patch up the wounds in my heart."

The man, the one I've truly always loved, nods his head, but his eyes are hard flint. "I know all of this. You don't think it guts me to hear that? That another man held my place while I lived my life, ignorant of the one I should have been a part of?"

"So we're back to this?" I huff, getting up in his face.

We're millimeters apart, just a technicality. With one breath, he could take my mouth. I hear the sounds of Mason's learning puzzle toy singing in the background and try to keep my voice down.

"You yelled at me about not being able to do the right thing. You said you should want to walk away, but you just couldn't. You don't see that it's the same for me? You don't think I want my family to be together? That I'd like something more than raising my son with the man who helped give him life? That I'd want anything else besides loving you for the rest of my days? It's a little more complicated than that, Vance. Or do you not remember you were the one who left me? You're the one who said it was better for us not to be together."

"Lara, how many times do I have to apologize? Because I'll do it. I'm the one who fired the first shot, but you started the war." His dimple kicks up when he grimaces, and I can't help but want to run my tongue over that, too.

Hurt, like the one he caused, doesn't just go away. But he's right. I'd made the decision to keep it from him and made the decision not to marry Louis.

"You're right." I hate admitting it. "We've both hurt each other. When you and I ended, it wasn't the end of my world. It was the end of the world I had with you. But then Mason became my world. He's an extension of you, a piece of you I got to keep, possibly a piece that you wouldn't have given if you'd had the choice."

"Again with this?" Vance throws his large, meaty hands up. "I told you not to bring those accusations against me. Especially now, when I clearly have so much love for our son."

I relent, sighing. "I'm sorry, that was a low blow. I just ... it's been a hard week."

"Tell me about it." Vance's eyes slide sideways, and we both hear Mason singing *"Wheels on the Bus"* in the other room.

I'm tired of fighting, and though it might not be the best idea, seeing as my fiancé just occupied this space not a day before, something in me gives up. Stops resisting. Allows my heart to follow itself instead of the bitterness in my brain.

"Mason would be happy to see you. Why don't you stay for supper?"

Vance looks about as shocked at the offer as I feel about extending it.

"All right. Thank you."

His eyes, the one I've dreamed about for years after he left, silently ask for one more chance.

20

VANCE

Lara's flat embodies everything I think of when I think of her.

It's warm and inviting, with a little bit of edge to it. Dark wood and leather highlighted by cream-colored rugs and curtains, with fixtures of iron or metal dotting the space. An abundance of houseplants give any guest visiting the feeling of walking into a forest, and I chuckle under my breath.

When we were together, Lara used to joke that she couldn't keep a bouquet of roses alive. I only gave her flowers once, and they were dead by my next visit just three days later.

Turns out, she's more nurturing than she ever gave herself credit for.

"Vance!" Mason shrieks as I walk into the living room, and a part of me can't wait for the day he calls me Dad.

"Hey, chap! I missed you. How was nursery school this week?" I pick him up, his tiny face nuzzling into mine, my nose pressed to his scalp. His scent can only be described as some addicting baby skin smell.

How can something this innocent and pure exist? Watching him, seeing the world through his eyes, it makes me want to be more open to every possibility. I suppose that's what happens when you become a parent.

"Der was giraffes!" he babbles excitedly, plucking the randomest of thoughts from his mind.

But his wonder for the world, his pure joy at just remembering a giraffe, or probably a drawing of one, makes my life brighter. I want to hear everything he has to say, watch on as he delights in the simplest of things.

I never thought I'd be inclined to take pleasure in watching a child swing at the park for hours on end. I was wrong. Before the blow-up with my parents, Lara let me take Mason to the playground for half an hour by myself the other morning, and all I'd done was push him in the baby swing for most of the time. He'd been absolutely chuffed.

"That's brilliant!" I tell him, setting him down. "What are you playing with?"

One look across the light colored carpet with a brown and red design running through it tells me that he's playing with everything. The entire stock of Hamley's might as well have thrown up on Lara's living room floor.

"Puzzles, um blocks, um football!" The little boy rattles off a few of the many playthings covering the floor beneath my feet.

"Well, we better get to it, then. Unless ... does your Mum need help in the kitchen?" I look to Lara.

It's the first time I've called her Mum in a third person way while speaking to Mason, and I can only imagine doing it for ... well, forever. The thought brands itself into my brain, and I know I'll be having dreams about a normal family life for weeks to come when I head back to Clavering tomorrow.

"I've got everything in here handled. You play."

For having just done some decent verbal sparring with each other, we were putting on ace faces for the lad. And even though it's probably misogynistic, I rather like hearing the sounds of

Lara cooking while I sit on the floor and play with our son. My stomach rumbles, reminding me that I've been waiting all day, nervous by my mobile, for her to call.

When she didn't, and I couldn't handle the suspense of whether or not her fiancé was still in the picture, I braved the monsoon going on outside to come over here.

Thirty minutes of Mason running around like an energizer bunny, showing me every toy he owns and insisting I color with him until the markers ran dry, and Lara is ready for us.

She places Mason in his high chair and offers me a seat next to him. After she brings over the teriyaki marinated chicken, broccoli, and wild rice she's prepared, she takes the seat on his other side. My throat goes dry and I feel a certain moisture collecting behind my eyes when I look at the picture in front of me.

My family, all seated at a dinner table, ready to share a meal.

When I glance over at the gorgeous woman across the table, I can read the same thought plain as day on her face. I want to memorize every inch of this moment, of the exact look that passes over those high cheekbones, the flush on them as she regards me too.

We eat with a bit of small talk interspersed, mostly us talking to Mason as he makes a mess out of himself. Half the time, the food barely makes it to his mouth, and he's so excited about the entire prospect of eating a meal with us that he's practically jumping out of his chair. He sings, stabs his fork on the tray, tries to tell me about the elephant he saw on the telly, and everything in between.

Lara and I smirk at each other the entire dinner, as she tries to shove food in his mouth without laughing at the hilarity of our little boy.

By the end of the meal, Mason is finally knackered, and almost falling asleep on the tray. Lara wipes him down, brushes his teeth in the chair, and then takes him out and hands him to me. Without protesting, I let his head droop against my chest as I follow her to the nursery that must be his.

It's done in blues and grays, with tiny sea creature and fishing boat decals on the wall behind the crib. In the corner is a bin full of stuffed animals, and I spot a regulation size Rogue FC soccer ball next to it. My eyes linger there, and I can feel Lara watching me as I stare at it.

All this time and there was evidence of me in my son's room.

"We have to get his diaper changed and him into pajamas," she whispers, because Mason is already quietly snoozing.

"Tell me what to do," I whisper back, wanting to take part in this nighttime ritual.

She instructs me through it, showing me and guiding my hands to change my first diaper. I strip off his messy dinner clothes and throw them in his hamper and make sure to wipe his bum extra carefully. Every body part is so small, a miniature human lying before me, trusting me to be gentle.

When he's in his pajamas, Lara lays a stuffed whale in his arms that he latches onto. "You can rock him a while if you want."

She points to a glider in the corner, and I willingly oblige, wanting so desperately to hold onto this sacred moment. Soon enough, he won't want to do this, even I know that with what little parenting knowledge I have. I missed so much of his life, if he allows me to sit and rock him, I'm going to take all the time I can get.

Lara leaves quietly as I prop my feet up on the swaying ottoman, and position Mason so he's laying against my chest comfortably. His face angles up, his eyes closed and breathing steady.

I just stare at him, that peaceful little face, as I silently gaze all of my hopes and dreams for him down into his features. I hope that he can learn to love me, that he feels the immense love I have for him. Someday, I hope I don't have to leave the house after he goes to bed.

The flat is bathed in darkness when I gingerly close Mason's door after laying him in his crib, and I find Lara in the kitchen. The sink, where she's washing dishes, muffles the sound of my arrival, and I get to just stare at her for a moment.

Wouldn't life be wonderful if I got to do this every night?

When I make it to her, resting my hip on the counter, I know it's time for the part of the conversation I don't want to have.

"I have to go back to the academy tomorrow." I duck my head, rubbing the back of my neck.

In the two weeks I've been on leave, I feel like I've accomplished nothing and everything. I made my intentions clear; I bonded with Mason, Lara broke off her engagement. My parents now know I have a son, and I've come to terms that I may never play for RFC.

But there is still so much to sort out. Lara is nowhere near ready to give us another go, Mason doesn't know I'm his father, nor has he met my parents. We haven't sat down to talk about what co-parenting will look like, or how much my schedule will allow me to be in Mason's life. And in terms of my professional career, that's floating somewhere in football purgatory.

"Oh," she says, a tinge of shock in her voice. "I didn't realize the time had gone so quickly."

"Yeah," I say because I don't know what else to say.

"When will you be back?" At least she's not celebrating my departure with a champagne pop as my car leaves town.

"I'm not sure. We have a ton of matches coming up, and there is a lot of uncertainty of where I might play. I have to figure something out, in terms of my career. But, I'm going to see Mason whenever I possibly can. I know that you might not want to make that easier, or for it to happen—"

Lara puts a hand up. "Vance, the one thing I won't interfere with is you seeing Mason. He is your son, and you deserve to nurture a relationship with him. If and when I can meet you halfway, or somewhere that works for a visit, I will do it."

A relieved breath huffs from my throat. "That means more than you know. I apologize, truly, Lara for all those times you drove out to meet me. I didn't appreciate it back then, I was so focused on myself that I couldn't see how much you sacrificed for me. I was a prick, a bloody bastard. I know you probably think I've been one the past two weeks, as well, but I have my reasons. This time, I'm thinking about the family we could have. I'm thinking about how no other woman in the world makes my heart want to soar out of my chest. You walk into a room and simply gut me, Lara."

"I need time, Vance." Her vibrant blue eyes plead with me.

"I know you do, love. I won't push." My words are gentle, and I want so madly to touch her.

"*Now* you won't push." She rolls her eyes, but in a good-natured way.

Sheepishly, I smile. "I've told you how I feel. You're single now. I can give you the space you need to figure this all out."

Before she can answer, because I'm all talked out and there isn't much else for us to say, I lean in and plant a lingering kiss on her forehead. My lips stay there for a second, and I hear Lara exhale a small sigh.

When I pull back, her blue eyes burn into mine.

"I'll message you tomorrow when I arrive in Clavering."

Even though every instinct in me is screaming to turn around, to not let my feet carry me out of her flat, I ignore them.

A change in tactics might work in my favor. If I respect her wishes, give her some time, perhaps she'll come around to my way of thinking.

21

VANCE

The main hall stands ominous and uninviting as I pull my rolling suitcases from the trunk of my car.

I used to get flutters in my stomach, electric jolts in my veins when I'd pull back onto the Rogue Academy grounds. This is my home, for all intents and purposes, and I was always excited to return.

But that was the past. Two of the main reasons I loved it here, Kingston and Jude, were now gone. I was the old bloke, compared to the lads here now, and I feel them hypothetically breathing down my neck at every turn.

I'm tired of living in a dormitory, showering with other men, and eating the gruel they serve in the dining hall. I want to sleep in a king bed with an expensive mattress, not a glorified full size with a rickety box spring.

I want to train in a real facility, and not be bored to death when coaches are going over the basics with younger players. I want to play in real matches, compete in the premier league and be a starter on the first squad.

I want to live with my son in my spare time, to have him be

proud of his daddy on the big stage. Most of all, I want to come home to Lara every night.

But, this is where I am for now. I've never been an impatient person, or one to jump the gun to get somewhere faster. I'll wait as long as I can, and when I can't stand it anymore, I'll make my move.

After unloading most of my things from my suitcases, I don a practice uniform, tie my boots, and head for the pitch. It's been too long since I put myself through a grueling, leg-murdering, head clearing practice.

The campus is shrouded in early winter; the frost clinging to the ancient windows and the gray gloom of low hanging clouds. The spires of the brown and gray church-like buildings that dot campus make the academy look more like one of the Queen's old palaces than a training ground for the future football stars of England.

I see the spot on a certain patch of lawn where Kingston once spray painted a knob and bollocks; it took the headmaster weeks to figure out it was him. Farther away, across the slope of a hill, is the sew house where Aria, Jude's fiancé, once worked. Another building reminds me of the tunnels we used to frequent beneath the grounds of the academy, where I lost my virginity one night while pissed off my arse.

Yes, this place had once been the breeding ground for all of our best pranks. And now, it's just empty for me.

There is a practice already in progress when I get down there, and I join in. As the most senior player here, I have free rein most of the time. It's common knowledge that I'll be the next bloke signed to a professional team, though if that's RFC is still to be determined. I'm one-third of the merry band of scoundrels, and most people around here still recognize me as such.

"Vance, good to have you back." Chester, one of the younger coaches, nods at me when I jog out onto the field.

I nod back. "Ready to work."

"Good. Let's make sure you can't walk after this." That evil gleam in his eye only spurs me on more.

The scent of the crunching grass beneath my feet gives me more of the familiar feeling of home, and as I kick my booted feet up in front of my body, I feel the tension leak from my bones. This is where I'm home. Not the academy, not in Brighton, not even in London where I long to be. With a pitch under my feet ... that's where I belong.

We run drills, cutting and passing and diving. These are mostly for positions farther up the pitch, but they're good for my endurance and knowledge of the game. If I can anticipate every move in my direction, I'll be that much better at blocking them.

I'm thankful for the hour of intense practice, because I have little time to think or worry over the shite hanging above my head.

"Time for penalty kicks!" A whistle screeches and one of the trainers yells.

My gut clenches, because this is my time to shine. Most players want nothing to do with being in goal. It's a thankless job, one that is never appreciated after a clean sheet, and one that is always blamed in a loss. But me? I relish it. Being a keeper is tough as shite, requires loads of composure and accuracy, and I get a rush out of the near-concussing experience of it all.

More than a dozen times in a match, there is a speeding football spinning revolutions toward my head and body. The natural instinct would be to move out of its way, to avoid being hit. As a keeper, I have to fight that flight mechanism in my system. I have to stand in its way, even move toward it, so I can keep my team in the match.

I love being the only thing standing in the way of an opposing player and his victory. I relish the feeling of crushing the enemy's dreams.

The academy players line up facing the goal, on the line that the trainer has specified. They're all under the age of twenty, and each has more testosterone and stamina than my old bollocks combined. They're raring to go, think I'm an easy target. The old bloke, the veteran ... surely they can beat me.

Oh, how wrong they are. I've been biding my time, reserving all of my pent-up anger and frustration for this right here. I may present a cool exterior, but inside, there is fire and poison whipping through my nerve endings.

"And, begin!" The whistle sounds again, and the first player winds up.

The football soars through the air, and he's gotten too much of his toe on it because it skies up past the net. *Naïve child with a premature boot*, I chuckle internally.

The next two are easy enough to defend, while I have to slide in the mud on the pitch to save a tricky ball at the last minute from a particularly young player. I punch one clear across the field, while two more players miss the goal entirely.

One of the sixteen-year-olds fakes left, but I calculated that, and I dive right as he tries to soar one past my earlobe. Using my hands as if they're an impenetrable brick wall, I bat it away. The ball rockets across the pitch as I come down hard, landing in the mud again. It cakes against my side, the frozen landscape cold and unyielding against my ribs.

Despite being banged around, adrenaline races through my heart and I feel better than I have in a week. The cathartic, aggressive act of facing a firing squad has me feeling back in my element. Confidence floods me.

"Vance, you're looking sharp. Perhaps the two weeks' leave

did you good." Headmaster Darnot comes from somewhere off the sidelines.

I hate this wanker, as do Kingston and Jude. He's done nothing but make our lives a living hell since we started at the academy. Every action has been under a microscope, and the git cares nothing about the chaps here. All he cares about is advancing his own agenda, which in this case is to get his name in every paper in London. Somehow, he's under the impression that a lackluster headmaster is going to be Rogue Football Club's savior.

"Thank you." I try not to grit my teeth as I say it.

"I'll have to report to Niles that you're looking ace." He gives me a conspiratorial grin. As if he's ever done me a favor in the last fifteen years.

"Swell," I clip.

His face sours. "You could show a little appreciation. The manager takes my recommendations very highly."

Right. It's a known fact that Niles tolerates Darnot because it means he doesn't have to oversee the academy as much.

"Yes, sir." My response is monotone.

He regards me with disdain, annoyance, and a hint of self-doubt behind his eyes, and then walks away.

Thank fuck. I don't want to put up with his antics on a good day, and I have so much on my mind right now that I'd have blown a gasket if he kept poking at me.

Plus, I've already made up my mind.

If and when Lara is ready to take me back, I am leaving the academy.

I'd do it now if she wasn't so hell-bent on needing space. But while she sorts her shite out, I'll still try to pursue my dreams with Rogue.

When she comes calling, though, I am out of here. My

family needs me more, and Niles Harrington and his minions have spurned me one too many times. My loyalty is quickly expiring.

I can play anywhere. But there is only one shot to get this right with Lara and Mason.

22

LARA

It only takes one week for pictures of Vance leaving my flat, and our son walking into daycare after that, to hit the media.

Apparently, someone in Brighton caught wind of our meetings, of how much time we were spending together, and tipped off the tabloids. The minute I saw Mason's face on some rubbish news site, I called Vance in hysterics.

We've been messaging back and forth in the days since he's gone back to Clavering. Mostly photos of Mason, updates on his practices, and just small talk. I haven't wanted to get into anything deep, and it looks like Vance is respecting what I said about needing space.

But this? I can't handle it. My child's face is all over the nation, with grown adults placing wagers on if Vance is actually the biological father. They're making horrible statements about me, about the relationship I have with the famous footballer. Calling me a kit chaser and saying my child is a bastard.

That one made my heart nearly crack in two.

My mind has been in a tailspin all morning.

"Look at what they're saying about him." My voice is a raw nerve.

"I agree, it's bloody awful. But these people are the scum of the earth, Lara. You can't listen to them. They shout shite for a living, the more exaggerated, the more they think they'll get paid."

Vance tries to reason with me, but this is beyond reason.

"I want to kill them," I rage murmur.

"I know. Believe me. If I could take a fist to this and solve a problem, I would. But, it will only make the situation worse. Retaliating, defending, or even trying to explain this to the media—it will all backfire. We're better off staying silent and allowing a professional to handle this. To contain the damage."

How can he be so rational? "Don't you even care what they're saying about you? About your son?"

On the other end of the line, he blows out a sigh. "Of course, it stings. What they're saying is vile, it's awful. But I've been dealing with them my entire life, so it gets easier to tune it out. And, you have to ask yourself: is what they're spewing true? I can't read your mind, we would avoid so many things if I could, but I don't think so. I'm not a deadbeat, they don't know the situation we're in or our past. Our son has two loving parents and loads more extended family who already love him or are ready to love him. He's brilliant, well cared for, and I'm cherishing every moment I get to be with him. Let their bullshit roll off your back. I know it's hard, but now that it's out there, at least we don't have to worry about someone finding out."

He does have a point, the two-year tension I've been carrying about keeping Mason's father's identity a secret is no longer threatening to break my shoulders. And I suppose, now that I've invited this chaos into my life by agreeing to a relationship—of what nature I still can't decide—with Vance, I have to deal with media exposés on my family.

After another five minutes of England's most serious footballer calming me down, which he's surprisingly good at, we finally ring off.

Mason has been down for a nap for an hour now, and I'm too anxious and jumpy to do anything but annihilate my house in a tidying spree.

Thank God for small miracles, because at least it's a Sunday. If I had to go into work today, if I had to face the evil mummy squad at Mason's nursery school I think I'd lose it even more than I already am.

About two hours after Mason wakes up, and my tidying has been ruined by his thousand-piece LEGO set dumped all over the floor, a knock at my front door spooks me. I am in the middle of devouring every news article I can find about my son and his father, which is the exact opposite of what Vance told me to do. In fact, the man told me to sit tight, not talk to anyone or go online, and that he's having a public relations expert handle this. As if it's that easy ... does he even know the things they are saying about us?

Paranoia steals over me as I walk quietly to the door, ready to pretend we aren't home if I look through the peephole and see someone I don't know.

But alas, it's just my mother. Which might be worse than a tabloid reporter.

I open it, and Mason spots her from where he's come to stand behind me in the hallway.

"Nanny!" he cries, rushing over on his stubby little legs to wrap her legs in a hug.

"Hi, darling." She scoops him up, planting kisses all over his cheeks. "What are you doing?"

Mason plays with the necklace she's wearing. "Playin' blocks!"

Everything my son says is said with enthusiasm, and a small

smile stretches my lips. If anything good comes from this day, it's spending it inside with him.

The chill from the early November air infiltrates my flat, and I usher Mum inside.

"To what do we owe this visit, Mum?" I ask as she sets Mason down, and he runs back to his toys.

"I got a call from Roberta Morley yesterday. I haven't spoken to her in some time, and out of the blue, she leaves a message on my mobile three days after I see Vance leaving town for the academy again."

Shite. Apparently, Vance hasn't shared the fact that his parent's now know my son is their grandchild. And clearly, my Mum has her suspicions.

"Is that right?" I ask, pretending to make myself busy tidying my flat. More than I already have today. Which is impossible.

"You know, I thought it was odd that Louis hasn't dropped Mason off at my house for the last week. Now I come here, and his car isn't out front …"

Is she going to make me admit everything to her? "Out with it, Mum. Don't play this coy game with me, I don't have the patience for it."

I wonder if she's seen the papers.

"And then, I was browsing around the Internet this morning, and found this." Mum pulls her iPad out of her bag, palming it so that the screen faces me.

Well, there is my answer. A side-by-side picture of Vance and Mason is splashed across the screen, the headline, "Rogue Backup Keeper has been Keeping His Son a Secret."

I want to punch the damn tablet.

"Bollocks," I mutter, knowing I'll have to hash this entire thing out with her.

"Were you ever going to tell me?" she poses the question.

I cross the room so that we're not shouting across the flat. The last thing I want is for Mason to hear.

"Didn't you already know?" I sigh, knackered from all the secret keeping.

Mum shrugs. "I suppose I had my suspicions. The boy looks eerily similar to our former neighbor. I'm just wondering why you never thought you could tell me."

"It's not like that, Mum. It has nothing to do with you, or my ability to trust you." Because I know that's what her wounded Mum-ego thinks. "When I got pregnant, it was obviously not planned. I was too young, too naïve, and I was also heartbroken. Vance and I had been together since I was sixteen, and he'd just broken up with me before I peed on that stick. I had no idea what I was going to do with a baby, but knew even less about what it would be like to co-parent with someone who had just slaughtered my heart. So I decided to keep it a secret. If he didn't know, if no one knew, then I wouldn't have to deal with all that messiness."

Mum looks over at Mason. "He really does look just like him."

"Don't I know it." I roll my eyes. "I spent nine months baking him, went through agony to deliver him, and he ends up looking just like that aggravating bloke."

"So, he was in town to ... what?" She's talking about Vance, and leave it to Mum to completely move past a subject she was just sour about.

To her credit, she's always been level-headed and easily able to accept an explanation at face value. It's what I admire most about her.

I sigh. "He saw Mason a couple months ago, by accident. I was on Main Street and I guess he was in town visiting his parents. Took one look at Mason and dropped the bag of wine bottles he was carrying. He took two weeks of leave from the academy to come sort things out. You could say it's been a challenging couple of months."

"I'm guessing that's why I haven't seen Louis in a while as well. And why you're no longer wearing your engagement ring?"

Damn, nothing gets past your mother, that's for certain.

"Do we have to go into all of this detail? You're my mother, you don't want to hear about the poor relationship choices I'm making."

Mum gives me a stern look. "Just because you're following you're heart, doesn't mean they're poor decisions. We make a lot of choices in life that hurt other people, mostly those closest to us, but it doesn't mean those choices aren't right. It doesn't mean they don't set us on a happier path."

And *wham*, she hits me with that sage wisdom again. "How is it that you always know exactly what to say?"

"I'm your mother, sweetheart. I was made for exactly this purpose. Someday, you'll do the same with him." She points at Mason, and we both linger our gazes over the content little boy playing on the rug.

"I broke it off. With Louis. I kissed Vance. Twice. And ... I knew I couldn't stay engaged to him. Not only was it wrong, what I'd done, but I didn't love him. Not the way you're supposed to when you're considering marrying someone." My heart aches with all the turmoil it's been through.

She nods. "At least you realized that *before* you got married. Turns out I did teach you one important lesson."

We spend the next hour and a half talking over the entire Vance-Mason-me saga, and Mum has a lot of advice interjected between my dramatic retelling. She always agrees with Vance on the ignoring the media front. Says nothing good will come from responding, or getting worked up by wankers.

By the time Mum leaves, I'm so mentally exhausted I could collapse on the entryway floor and fall into a deep sleep. But no,

I still have supper, bath time and his bedtime routine to get through.

Thankfully, Mason doesn't fight me much during it all. He eats the lasagna I prepared, doesn't fuss when he's asked to climb out of the tub, and quietly nuzzles into my arms as I read him *The Giving Tree*.

"Luf you, Mummy," he whispers as I rock him gently against my chest, swaying my way toward the crib.

And even though today went to piss, those three words erase it all. All the fear, anger, worry, and doubt I have floating around in my chest, they just cease to exist.

As long as my boy is okay, as long as he can sleep peacefully with love in his heart, then I'll be okay, too.

Mason goes down without a peep, and I walk to the dining table in the middle of my flat. Plopping down, I spend a good five minutes just staring off into space. I need the wind down time, the quiet with my thoughts before I attempt to clean the dishes, pack our bags for tomorrow, and slink off to bed.

When I'm done drowning in my sorrows, I pull myself up, complete my tasks, and change into pajamas. Just an hour of mindless reality television on the couch won't hurt, and it might just cheer me up marginally.

What I don't expect is the doorbell ringing the moment I spread a blanket over my lap. I also don't expect my ex-fiancé to be standing on my stoop when I open the door.

"Vance fucking Morley, Lara?" Louis stalks into the flat, not pausing once to check if this is a good time.

"Christ, Louis, do you know what time it is? And don't use that language in here. You're lucky Mason is sleeping. I thought you were in Wales?"

I have to rub the sleep from my face because he's shown up right when I was about to head off to bed.

"Have you seen the papers? Mason's face is splashed bloody

everywhere. Alongside Vance's, of course. But you already knew that. Almost three years, Lara, and you couldn't have bloody told me that the bloke who knocked you up was England's next great keeper?"

Louis is irate, bitter anger pouring off of him in waves, and his tone with me is cruel. He's looking at me like I'm some kind of gutter rat.

"And here I thought you loved me out of the goodness of your own heart, and wanted to care for my son like your own," I spit back.

Don't expect to show up at my house close to midnight, accuse me of being a slag, and then think I'm going to take it lying down simply because I recently broke your heart. Louis should know me better than that. After everything I've been through, tough is the only thing I can count on being.

"Vengeful, are we? Imagine my surprise when I find out my fiancé—I'm sorry, ex-fiancé. Imagine my surprise when I find out you were shagging some athletic superstar and never told me. Were you a kit chaser the entire time we were together?"

That feels like a slap in the face, even if he hasn't physically touched me since he stormed in.

"Don't. You. Dare." Each word is clipped.

"I look like a bloody idiot, Lara. My friends and family are calling me with millions of questions about Mason, you, and Vance fucking Morley."

"It's none of their business. And at the time, it wasn't yours either. Not that I owe you an explanation, what with how you're speaking to me, but I had no contact with Vance from right after I got pregnant till a little over two months ago. I'm not a slag, I was faithful to you and tried to build a life with you."

"Up until you kissed him behind my back. Did I get that timeline right?" Louis is furious, but something else seems off.

"Are you drunk?" I think I smell cigarettes on him as well.

"What does it matter to you? I'm a single man now, I don't have to answer to anyone."

I try to take a calming breath, to put myself in Louis's shoes. His life has been upended, and now he gets this news. And it wasn't even straight from my mouth. I can only imagine how much shock and hurt he's feeling right now.

"I should have told you. I apologize for that. But until you can come here with a clear head, and calm emotions, we can't discuss this. Mason is sleeping in the next room. Don't do this, Louis. Just go. Get home safe."

His eyes are still full of spite, but at least I see some regret filter through them. "We will talk about this. And I want time with my son."

I nod, trying to herd him to the door. With one last angry look over his shoulder, Louis stalks out.

It won't be the end of his upset with me, nor I fear, his claim over Mason.

Could nothing in my life ever just be simple?

23

LARA

My knuckles are white as they grip the steering wheel.

If I wait in my car any longer, Mason will be late for school, and that will just be another mark against me as a mother.

But I've tried to take count of all the mum's holding the hands of their children, escorting them into the red brick building. If I can be the last one in, I can avoid any run-ins with judgmental shrews who don't know any of my business but feel they can speak on it anyway. I'm sure the gossipers of Brighton are having a field day now that they all know the real identity of my child's father.

Not that I care. I learned long ago not to let the sting of their judgment invade my thoughts. I've grown a thick skin to the insults, side-eyes, comments that I'm trash … so why can't I seem to do it when it comes to the tabloids?

Perhaps because they don't know me or my son at all and seem to have an opinion on our characters.

"All right, here goes nothing," I say to myself, opening the door and stepping out into the frigid air.

There's something about living by the ocean in the winter months that makes it that much colder. The salty, moisture-filled air smacks at my cheeks and hair, invading my bones with its icy fingers.

Mason is occupied with a stuffed Mickey Mouse toy when I reach in to unlatch his seatbelt, and he protests coming out into the cold.

"I know, love. But we'll be inside soon, with your friends." I hug him close to me, shouldering my purse and throwing my keys inside.

I bustle up the sidewalk, trying to transfer any warmth I might have over to my son. He giggles as I speed walk because he's jostling in my arms and thinks it's a game.

Just as I'm about to step the final way toward the front door, I almost slam right into another body.

My head snaps back as I halt my progress, grabbing Mason extra hard to me to keep both of us upright.

"Oh, Lara." Portia stands just before me, blocking the entrance to the school.

She's in a posh outfit, with heels that only a barmy bird would wear in this weather, and wears a snarky grin on her face.

"Morning," I mumble, gritting my teeth and squaring my shoulders. "Just trying to bring Mason inside before he freezes. Excuse me."

She doesn't budge. "Listen, Lara, it's just awful what's happening in the press. You must be downright depressed. What with Vance Morley not claiming your son, and now Louis has left you."

Her eyes scan my left hand, and I can't help the ashamed blush that steals over my cheeks. This *witch*.

"That's not the case at all." I leave it at that, knowing that even if I did, an explanation wouldn't stop her from chomping at the rumor bit.

"It must be hard to keep all these blokes straight. Although, being such a young mum means your brain might be a bit sharper. You have taken secondary school maths more recently than I have."

Wow. *Ouch.* That one nearly pierced the flesh. An attack on my age, since I had Mason so young.

"You're right. My brain is sharper." I choose to use her words against her.

"Perhaps. Now that you're no longer planning a wedding, what with your baby daddy drama, maybe you'll have more time to volunteer here with Mason's class. We could really use you pulling your weight."

How she can, in good conscience, say these things in front of my son is just unfathomable. But that's the thing, isn't it? Portia doesn't have a good conscience. Honestly, it's downright rotten.

I'm too stunned to speak, and if I thought the backlash from Brighton's residents finding out who my son's father is was going to be bad I underestimated more than slightly.

"Cheers." She smirks, striding away, and I want to claw her eyes out.

Not worth it, not worth it, not worth it. I try to repeat this over and over as I seethe, but it would be *completely* worth it. The only thing stopping me is Mason in my arms.

"Mummy? No wedding?" he quips in my ear.

Fuck. She had to go there? "Hush, sweetheart, let's go play!"

I hurry into the school. Hopefully, by the time I pick him up, he'll have forgotten all about our run-in with evil Portia.

I'm pouring myself a glass of cabernet after putting Mason down, when my mobile rings.

I deserve a whole bottle's worth of wine for what I've had to endure today, but since I'm the only one home if something goes wrong with Mason, I'll savor this slightly overfilled glass.

"Hello?" I say as I put the phone on speaker.

I saw Vance's name on the display, but still find it strange he's calling me after Mason's gone to bed. Not that we haven't texted, we've shared more messages than just about our son. For his part, my ex-boyfriend has given me the respect not to push the envelope on the whole "I love you, I want to be with you, we have an undying passion until the end of time," thing.

"Hi."

And I feel pissed already. That's what one word from Vance can do.

"How was your day?" he grumbles, his rough voice needling at my core.

It's been about two weeks since he left, and I've fantasized about him every night. No wonder, what with the man being sex on a six-foot stick.

Taking my glass of wine, I mosey to the couch, taking a long sip while sinking down into the cushions.

I snicker. "You may not want to ask that."

A rustling comes from the other end, and my imagination pictures Vance getting comfortable in his bed, or on a couch. I picture that big body, preferably shirtless, adjusting until his hand is resting on his abdomen, the hair and muscles flexing beneath it.

I don't drink much, so this wine must have already gone to my head if I'm having sexual fantasies about Vance while we're actively talking on the phone.

"Uh oh, what happened?" He sounds genuinely concerned.

"Oh, just mean mums at Mason's school. Judgy, psychotic slags," I huff out.

"Those wankers don't know anything. Don't listen to them. You're an incredible mum."

Always a succinct talker, but the things he does say are so meaningful.

"Thank you." I blush. "How was your day?"

"Eh, it was fine. Had practice. Ate, went to the physical therapist. I just want to get the fuck out of here."

It's the first time I've ever heard him speak ill of the academy. It's only now that I realize I barely asked Vance anything about his life when he was in Brighton for those two weeks.

"What do you mean, get out of there?" I'm curious.

His life has been football since the time I met him, and it's surprising to me that he's almost talking rubbish on it now.

"I've been here since I was eight, and I'm an aging veteran at best. All the blokes I trained up with are gone, either to Rogue or sold to other teams. They're competing, they're playing through their best football years. I'm sitting in this bloody academy as a backup keeper because they're too selfish to let me go play elsewhere. I'm biding my time for Remus to get hurt, or finish his contract, or want to play for a different team. I'm in football purgatory, and I'm ready to start. These bloody arses just won't let me. My loyalty only runs so deep."

Blimey, I've never heard him talk about Rogue like this before. Back when we were together, he'd have thrown himself on a bloody grenade for that football club. But I understand it. He wants to play, that has been his dream all along. It must be torture to watch Jude, Kingston, and all the other mates he's gone to academy with playing on a worldwide stage.

My heart breaks for him, because no one works harder or deserves a place on the pitch more than Vance. I might not be ready to give him another shot romantically, but I can admit that he's one hell of a footballer without any reservation.

"You shouldn't sit back and let them do that to you, then. For as long as I've known you, you've been nothing but steadfast and focused in pursuit of playing in the premiership, and that's what you should do. Tell those people to bugger off, and get the job you want. I believe in you."

That last bit popped out of my mouth without warning, and I want to suck it back in because it means I feel something personal in the situation. Which I do, but I'm not ready for Vance to know that.

"Thanks, Lara." There is a pause, and I think we both know I just showed him the first bit of kindness in a while. "Aside from the mean mums, is Mason okay?"

I can't tell him about Louis storming over here the other night. If I do, it will do nothing but make him go all aggro and blow back into town with vengeance on his mind. I don't need a brawl, or to be rescued. What I do need is his head on straight, because aside from the leaking of his parentage to the media, we have loads more to figure out.

"Yes, he's oblivious to it all. Happy as a clam. In fact, he keeps asking if you'll take him to the park again."

"Is that so? I'll have to get back stat." I can almost hear Vance's smile in his words.

"Your presence wouldn't be unwelcome." I'm not sure where I'm going with that, but it's not just Mason who wants to see him again.

"Is that so?" His voice has dropped an octave, and if I'm not mistaken, I'd say Vance Morley is flirting.

"Maybe if you bring that cheese on toast I used to love from that place in Clavering, I'll even compliment you." He used to bring a sandwich that had gouda and bacon stuffed between thick toast, and I'd give my left breast for it right now.

"Only if I'm allowed to stay and eat one with you. Alone." He throws down the gauntlet.

"I wouldn't object to that." I bite my own fist after I say it.

Here I am, sitting in the flat that I rent with my own money, legally drinking a glass of wine while my child sleeps in the next room, and I feel the same flutter of lustful, exciting flirting that I did when I was sixteen.

How Vance makes me feel this way, like I'm riding a roller coaster with rose-colored glasses, I'll never understand. Because I can't seem to feel this way about anyone else.

"Think about what I said, Lara. My feelings haven't changed. I'm still just as in love with you as I was when we were teens."

I'm pretty sure he rings off before I can say anything; he probably fears I'll turn him down again.

Mental, though, that he knows exactly what I'm thinking.

24

VANCE

Sweat drips from my brow, almost freezing on the hair.

The stark contrast of my body temperature against the icy air leaves my fingers numb and my entire face chapped from the wind, but I barely notice.

There are only seconds left in stoppage time, and my squad is barely hanging onto our one goal lead.

"Mark your man!" I scream, steering the ship from in front of the net.

Not only is my job to literally stop the other team from scoring a goal, but as keeper I'm the eyes of the team. I watch everything with laser focus, calling out to my strikers, forwards, and backs to tell them when they're about to get passed, tripped up, or outrun. My expertise is to keep us in formation, keep us formidable so that I don't become the last line of defense before that ball sinks into the back of my net.

And today, that part of my job has been harder than ever. I miss the days when my academy squad played so in sync that I rarely had to command anyone. When Jude and Kingston played with me, we functioned as a sole unit, almost sharing one brain.

These new blokes are clumsy and inexperienced. Cocky little shites, too. They don't listen, hog the ball, and try to outrun everyone to the point that they're winded. I suppose, at one point, we were like them. But then we grew up, moved on.

Well, some of us have moved on.

"Stay on top of him! Don't let him ... *bloody hell!*" My ire rings out across the pitch as an opposing player comes barreling toward me.

The arrogant prick on my squad has terrible footwork and was an easy defeat for the player about to shoot the ball directly at my face. I hear the smattering of supporters in our bleachers cry out because it would be useless if we lost the game after being up for more than half of it.

My heart jumps into my throat, but my leather-gloved hands go to the ready. I stare him down, knowing that sooner or later, he'll be kicking that speeding orb right at my body.

He winds up, and I crouch, adrenaline shooting through my feet. The ball comes hurdling toward my net, my zone. I spring sideways, reaching endlessly, endlessly ...

It twirls just past my fingertips, brushing the very end of my glove as it sinks into the white string behind me.

"Fuck!" I scream as my body hits the ground.

Pain radiates through every cell, but again, I don't feel it. All I feel is the slice of disappointment cutting through every muscle, tendon, and bone. I may loathe being at the academy, but it doesn't mean I don't give one hundred and ten percent through everything I do.

Football players hate to lose, but I more than hate it. I despise it. Each time a tally is marked in the lost column against me, I sink into a deep funk. Sometimes for days. Kingston and Jude used to have to take me to the local pub and get me legless before I could put the defeat behind me.

"Tough loss, but you played well, mate." The git who let the winning goal get by him pats me on the shoulder.

I want to break his hand.

There will be post-game meetings and film sessions, and some of the squad will go eat in the dining hall together. I want no part of it. I head back to my empty dorm room and punch the wall of my shower so hard that I think I crack one of the tiles.

It's not planned, but I've had such a shite day that the only thing I know will make me feel better is two hours away. Without telling any administrators where I'm going, or concerning myself with what Rogue will think about my departure, I get in my car and begin driving.

It's a tad comical that the only thing I used to look forward to was practice and matches. I breathed, ate, and slept football. If my squad lost, it would gut me. But now, there is something I long for more than football.

My family.

Two and a half hours later, with flowers in one hand and a giant lollipop in the other, I ring the door for Lara's flat.

Muffled stomping comes from the other side, and in a moment, Lara is opening the door.

Mason darts out, hugging my legs. "Vance!"

"What ... did you just get into town?" Lara looks surprised, but not in a way that I'm scared she might throw me off her doorstep.

"Had a bad loss today. Just wanted to see you guys," I give her the simple explanation.

"Well, come on in. That is, if you can detach the dinosaur from your leg." Lara makes a motion of play-attack toward Mason, who is suctioned around my calf.

He shrieks and stumbles off, running in a way only a toddler can.

"Thanks. I didn't know if you'd be open to this. But you were the only thing I could think of that would cheer me up." I put emphasis on the word *you*, trying to make it clear that I want to see her, aside from our son.

Lara looks edible in her tight black lounge pants, plain baby blue long sleeve that matches her eyes, and her hair twirled up on the top of her head. Her face is free of any makeup, not that she needs it. With long natural lashes and a pert little mouth, I think about all the ways I can unwind with her when Mason goes off to bed.

fter another dinner as a family, which lifts my spirits more than I ever thought it could, Lara and I put Mason to bed.

"Do you want a glass of wine?" she asks, moving to pull two glasses down.

"That would be brilliant." I nod, crossing to her couch.

I'm going to have to find a hotel for tonight, I can't go to my parents. If I go there, they'll only drill me with questions about why I'm in town, if they can meet their grandson yet. I've been holding them at bay, but I can feel Mum's annoyance growing by the day. No, I've had enough frustration in the last twelve hours, better not to venture home.

Lara brings the glasses over. "Cheers."

"Cheers," I mutter, never breaking eye contact as we drink.

"I still remember what you told me about breaking eye contact over a sip." She smiles to herself, and if I'm not mistaken, I think I see a blush creep up her cheeks.

"Oh, yeah?" I try to lace some charm into my voice.

"No one wants seven years of bad sex." Those blue eyes dart to the side, and she hastily takes another drink like she's said too much.

"No. They don't."

My sex drive screams in my ears, *kiss her, kiss her*. He's raring to go and it's the first time I've gotten Lara alone, in a situation where she might not bite my head off, since I started pursuing her again.

But I can't. It's not the right time. I still have no idea where her thinking is at about us.

"Should we talk about a custody agreement? Or visitation schedule?" It has been a few weeks since I confessed my feelings, and Lara hasn't reciprocated.

I know we can't keep going like this, that at some point the camel's back is going to break. It's better to have a plan in place. And if that plan isn't going to be me wooing her back, then I have to be smart for my son.

Lara blinks, and I can feel the warmth of her hand laying so close to mine on the back of the couch. I take a sip of wine, the rich red invading my brain with a haze.

"Why would we need to do that?" Her voice is quiet.

"To protect ourselves. So I can protect myself." My words are barely above a whisper.

"I wouldn't keep him from you." Lara's eyes don't leave mine.

"I don't think you would. But you never know. If this isn't … if you and I—"

What I'm trying to say is that if she decides she doesn't want to try to fall in love with me again, then we have to have rules. Somewhere down the line, as much as my hands ball into fists at the thought, one of us could find someone else. Who knows what a man dating her would say about Mason's biological father always dropping in unannounced.

"What if … what if I want to try?"

Breathing ceases to be an activity my body can perform.

"Do you?" I choke out on my last bit of air.

"Yes." The word almost isn't audible.

Our mouths are so close now, with every uttered piece of speech we lean in farther. I can feel her breath on my lips, feel the tiny hairs that stand up on her hand.

Lara clears her throat, then downs the last of her glass. "You can stay here if you want. On the couch. It's late. I'll get you some blankets."

And with that, she stands up, breaking the moment.

She wants to try. Lara is open to, what? Dating me? It seems like such a juvenile word with all that we've been through.

But if juvenile is what I get, it's what I'll take.

After all, we did our best work as juveniles.

25

LARA

"I'm going to ask your mummy on a date tonight."

I hear this from where I stand, opening the post, at the small table I have near the front door.

Um, what?

Mason is babbling when I walk in to the two of them cuddled up on the couch, *Sesame Street* playing on the TV.

"Mummy date Daddy." He grins.

Vance seems to stumble over that word. "Well ... er ... yes. Your mother is going to be dating your father, but Mason, I'm not sure you quite understand—"

"What's this about a date?" I interject hastily, not wanting Vance to be the one to explain the birds and the bees to our son.

That thick head of midnight black hair shoots up, and per usual, it's an electric jolt to the heart to behold Vance's face. All of those sharp angles, strong jawline, cleft chin, and bugger, those eyes. It's impossible not to stare at him, to think about him, with all of that to fancy.

"Elmo funny!" Mason giggles, and Vance lights up like a Christmas tree.

He may not know how rewarding it is to hear your toddler

speak for the first time, but it's clear that the gorgeous man cuddling our son on my sofa is enamored by the phrases Mason is putting together.

Oh, and that adorable dimple that appears whenever he smiles? Blimey, it makes me weak in the knees.

It took everything in me to stay in my own bed last night. When Vance had shown up at our door unexpectedly, I won't lie and say my heart didn't skip two beats. So when I knew he was lying on my couch, all of those muscled limbs stretched out just feet away from me; I think I stared at the ceiling awake most of last night.

"Make sure he listens to them counting," I instruct before going back to my post sorting.

"Sorry about that. I didn't mean ... I wasn't going to suggest he call me his father." He looks apologetic as he walks up to me.

It's a complicated situation. Most times, when a single mum starts dating again, she's cautious about introducing her children to a new man. There is the awareness of not trying to replace their father, or the slow slide it takes to acquaint another male role model into their lives.

But with Vance and Mason, it's a whole new playing field. Because he actually *is* his father. How am I supposed to explain to my son, who is under two years old, that he can no longer think about Louis, the man who raised him since birth, as his father? How am I supposed to force him to call Vance "Daddy," or institute the relationship when he's so used to having Louis around?

It's a mess, is what it is. I haven't figured out which path to take, much less begin to go down it.

Not that Louis is making much of a case for staying in Mason's life. Honestly, I'm disappointed. I really thought that they had their own special bond, regardless of what our romantic involvement was. But, I haven't heard from Louis since the night he stormed over and confronted me about Vance being Mason's biological father. Mason hasn't asked after his whereabouts, and that strikes a note of sadness inside me.

It makes me feel like a rotten mum for being, well, almost happy that Louis isn't trying to come around. If I don't have to juggle the both of them, Mason will just be left to turn to Vance as his father figure. That makes me horrid, doesn't it?

"It's all right. I just ... I want to take things slow. But, a date sounds nice." I give him a small smile.

"Well, I have to admit, it won't be that eventful. I thought I could order in takeout from Pucci's, since Mason will be sleeping here. I just ... I don't want people to know I'm in town."

My heart dims a little. Here I thought we were starting over, trying to have a normal relationship this time through. And he's suggesting staying in, hiding in my flat, instead of showing our neighbors that we're together.

Instantly, Vance's eyes flood with panic. "No, Lara, that's not what I mean. Of course, I want to take you *out* out. Believe me, if I could drive you to London right now I would book a reservation at the poshest restaurant in town. But with all the tabloid stories, I thought it would be better to protect Mason if we just stayed in. It's just sensitive right now, and I want as much time with the two of you in private before the media begins invading our lives again."

Oh. Well, that *does* make sense. "As long as you're not repeating the patterns we set up in our relationship way back when."

Vance does something unexpected, bridging the gap between us and pulling me into a hug. Thus far, he hasn't even attempted to make another move after our kiss that ended my engagement.

That's always been Vance, though, making the move when you least expect it. It throws my heart for a loop, and I can't help but melt into the embrace. His muscles twitch under the arms I have wrapped around his tapered waist, and I wish I didn't have to think so much before getting naked with him. Because right now, with all of my parts pressed against all of his, a sharp need pulses in my core. It reminds me just how desperate I've always been for Vance.

He groans into my hair, and I know that he's taking this chance to feel every curve of my body over my clothes. A fire starts low in my belly, my thighs itching with anticipation, though I know we can't do anything about it right now.

Large callused fingers tip my chin back, his hand maneuvering my jaw so I have to look up at him.

"I promise you, I will never put you in the background again."

Again, it's a simple statement. But if Vance looks you in the eye and says something, then he genuinely means it.

We stare into each other's eyes for another minute or so.

"So, how's about that date? I'll settle for pad Thai on the living room floor. It'll be the cheapest night you'll ever have?"

26

VANCE

Mum and Dad stand in the entryway to their house holding hands.

Or more gripping hands, because both of them look as if they might spontaneously combust if either of them lets go.

"Can you two calm down, please?" I try to keep my voice level, but they've gone mental.

"This is a big day, darling. I'm just so nervous." Mum wipes her free hand on her pant leg and smiles at me nervously.

"I know it is. But don't fret, he's a friendly little lad."

They've been asking me for weeks if they can meet my son. Messaging, calling, trying to sneak the idea through Harlow. My sister has talked to me more in the last month than she has in well, probably all the years she's been alive. And after our "date" last night, I finally convinced Lara to let my parents meet Mason.

This morning, I let them know I'm in Brighton, and here we are, just hours later. It's going to be an awkward interaction, but I'm also excited. My parents are good, loving people, and I have no doubt they'll love their grandson as much, if not more, as they do their children.

I also want them to see how my small family of three interacts. I know they're not pleased with Lara, but this is the woman I plan to spend my life with. They're going to have to move past this obstacle.

Last night, Lara and I had a feast of Thai food delivered. We spread it out on the floor, lit a candle on the coffee table, sat on pillows and just talked.

Out of anyone I've ever met, the only person who gets me to open up like she does is Lara. I'm usually not conversational, but something about sitting across from her makes me want to flirt, listen, and tease. Not a lot of people would call me a charming bloke, but when I'm with Lara, it's a different story.

We talked for hours, about everything and nothing. She told me about teaching, about how she got to instruct students on the books she's always loved. She told me the story of Mason's birth, when he took his first steps, the way he spit out carrots the first time he tried them. I told her about all the shite I'm going through at the academy, and how I've worked out at the Brighton facilities. Not that I want to get her hopes up, but with every passing second spending time with them in their flat, I want to be here full time.

And then we got into deeper conversation. Lara opened up to me about how lost she felt after I left. How stricken she was when she took that pregnancy test and knew she couldn't come to me. It gutted me to think about that young, fiery bird I knew feeling so alone. I admitted to her that I was a daft idiot, that I was trying to protect my own heart rather than work through our issues.

But we were young, we both agreed on that. I didn't tell her this, but maybe we were working out exactly the way we were supposed to.

The doorbell rings, and it's Dad who jumps up to answer it.

"Ann Marie, so good to see you. It's been too long," he says as he swings the door open.

Standing on my parent's front step are Lara, Lara's mother, Ann Marie, and Mason. Lara has Mason's nappy bag slung over her shoulder, and Mason is bouncing on the balls of his feet.

"Ocean?" He looks up at me and asks, because he remembers being here when we played on the beach.

"Sure, we can go out to the ocean. You'll have to bundle up again." I crouch down and spread my arms, and my son walks into them for a hug.

I turn my head when I hear a gasp from across the room.

Mum looks like she might faint. Or cry. I can't quite tell which. She and Dad are staring at Mason as if he might open his mouth and my voice will come out.

"Blimey, he's you as a toddler," Mum whispers.

I nod. "He does look a lot like me."

"You carry them for nine months and they come out looking like their father," Lara quips.

It's a rather bold statement, seeing as she may be on thin ice with my parents. I'm sure we're all going to have an awkward discussion later about why she kept their grandson from them for a year and a half.

"Hello, Mason. I'm your grandpa." Dad bends down to get eye level with my son.

Mason tilts his small head, regarding this new grown up in front of him. "Pa?"

Dad nods enthusiastically. "Brilliant. I'll be Pa. Would you like to go see the presents your nana and I bought for you?"

He stands, offering the toddler his hand.

"Presents!" Mason throws his hands up and then eagerly accepts my father's hand, the two of them walking off deeper into my parent's house.

"Good to know that all he needs to be lured away is the mention of presents." Lara chuckles.

"That boy sure does love a good gift." Ann Marie smiles.

"Please, come in," I say while ushering them into the house, because apparently my mother has lost her ability to speak.

I'm not sure I've ever witnessed this in my life.

Mum stares after Dad and Mason as if she's seen a ghost.

Ann Marie walks to her and lays a hand on her arm. There is a smile in her voice when she speaks. "It's quite a shock, right?"

"You could say that. I had no idea." Mum turns her head to look at Lara's mother.

Something passes between them, a look of experienced motherhood and shared ... pain? I suppose it's because Lara kept this secret from us all. For good reason, but she still did so. The rest of us are still adjusting to our new reality.

"Would you like to go meet your grandson?" Ann Marie extends her hand, wanting my mother to take it.

Mum nods, but pauses, turning to Lara. "Thank you for bringing him over here. I have to admit, I'm not pleased with how long it's taken. But you are his mother. Someday soon, I'd like to sit down. But right now, I think ... yes, I'd like to go spend the afternoon with my grandson."

Lara nods, her face somber.

We're all going to have wounds to patch up, reasoning to understand. It won't be easy, *bloody hell* it's going to be incredibly hard I figure. But at least we're all here, trying to come together for Mason.

So, that's what we do. My mum walks in and sits down on the rug, and my parents along with Lara's mum spoil Mason rotten for the next three hours.

27

LARA

The next month flies by, and between the end of term at school and juggling my home life, I can barely see straight.

Most weeks, I'm flitting about to remain an ace teacher and mum at the same time. Without Louis around, I'm handling a lot more than I used to, and it's not as if I can ask Vance to take his half of the load. He's still at the academy, though I sense his loyalty will run out shortly.

At least I have his parents on my side now; Roberta has been instrumental in keeping my life on track. She picks Mason up from nursery school on days I need to stay late at school, grade papers, or plan lessons. She came over to stay with him while he napped last week when I had to go to a baby shower for a friend. And in general, Vance's parents have been almost splendid about it all.

There was the one conversation we all had, while my mum watched Mason in the other room. Roberta and Mason's father, Kip, sat across from Vance and I at their dining room table, silent as church mice. I could practically hear their reproachful glares, or maybe I was imagining it. Roberta began to cry and asked what they'd done that I kept this from them. I tried to explain, without going through the details of mine and Vance's breakup with a fine-tooth comb, that it was very complicated. But that I'd never meant to hurt them. That I'd done it to preserve Mason's heart and not break theirs. I admitted that I cocked up, that the decision I made gutted them and apologized for that.

Kip was the one who patted my hand, who dried his wife's tears, who took the position that perhaps it was best to leave the past in the past. When he said that, something clicked in my brain. I'd been spending an awful lot of time dwelling there, the past that is, and not enough time realizing all the things Mason now gained by having the other half of his biological family in his life.

I also wasn't spending enough time trying to move forward with Vance. For so long, the bitterness that had clouded my heart due to the nature of our breakup ... well, it blinded me. Perhaps it was just best to let that hurt lie in the past and build a new future.

And that's what I've been trying to do. Which is why Vance is spending Christmas at our flat. Our first Christmas as a family, Mason is practically over the moon.

"Mummy, open presents?" Mason asks from where he's lounging with his stuffed whale on the couch.

"Not until tomorrow morning, love," I tell him for the fiftieth time.

Because when you're under the age of two, it's torture to see presents you can't open sitting there with all of their shiny bows.

It's the first Christmas that he'll really understand what's going on, or at least I hope so, so I've gone all out. The flat looks like St. Nicholas and his elves did a practice run for decorating the North Pole, and it glimmers with all the Christmas magic a child is supposed to have when they're this young.

"Maybe just one." Vance smirks, and I glare at him.

He's been pushing the boundaries lately, flexing his parenting muscles. Honestly, it's a little bit refreshing. I love being a mum, and I've always done most of the rule setting, schedule keeping, and consequence doling, even with Louis. After all, I was his only biological parent. But now Vance is here, and he's taking to the whole dad thing like a natural.

The other day, when Mason threw a tantrum over a block not fitting right on another block, Vance ignored his outburst and then rewarded him with a cuddle when Mason finally stood up and dried his tears on his own. Vance has also gotten the dinnertime sternness down, and Mason actually ate a few green beans for him the other day.

We still haven't told Mason that Vance is his real father. Not only am I sure that he won't understand what that truly means, but I think it's too soon. Too soon after Louis walked out of his life. Too soon for Vance and me since we're just figuring out how we fit together again. Just, too soon.

I roll my eyes. "How come I always have to play bad cop?"

"Because I like it when you're bad," Vance says in my ear as he passes me on his way to the tree.

Oh, *about* that. While there has been a lot of kissing and heavy petting, we haven't gotten much past that stage. Although I'm not sure I can hold him off for much longer. Vance has always been a beast when it comes to shagging, I remember weekends when we were first dating where we'd rarely get out of bed. He's been respectful of not pushing me,

but I'm about ready to push myself over that hump. Pun intended.

Things have been brilliant between us since I changed my mindset, and I finally feel ready to give this a real go.

"All right, one present, and then we have to put out carrots for the reindeer and cookies for Santa, and then it's off to bed," I hastily say, hoping to rouse him from the couch and into bed quickly.

Mason sits in Vance's lap as he tears into his one Christmas Eve present, which turns out to be a shirt with different kinds of dinosaurs on it. He loves it, but looks longingly at the pile under the tree, most of which are toys and he picked the one present that contained clothing. His father scoops him up, carts him to the kitchen to lay out cookies that I will bite into later, and then we hustle him into bed.

For as fun as the holidays are, I'm bloody exhausted and tomorrow will be a marathon. I love the joy on my child's face, but trying to keep my energy at peak levels all day will leave me knackered.

"When do we get to eat the cookies?" Vance asks, walking to where I stand at the tree with cookies already in hand.

"Hm, I suppose you found your answer."

"You made my favorite." Vance grins as he bites into a Hershey kiss thumbprint cookie.

"With extra peanut butter in the batter," I confirm. "They're your son's favorite, too."

"Smart chap, he is," the dishy man says around cookie crumbs as he gazes at the star atop the evergreen.

We stand next to the tree, the lights twinkling next to us, clogging my vision with romantic holiday notions and magic. It's impossible not to overflow with compassion at Christmas; it's a softer time, putting even the Scrooges in a charitable mood.

Perhaps that's me, the Scrooge of this relationship. Vance has been nothing but a gentleman and a staunch support system. Even from afar, he's always checking in on us. When he's here, he's always offering to take Mason off my hands or run errands for me. He cleans, to cook, and even takes my rubbish bins out. He communicates, doesn't disappear for days, and has even taken me on a few public dates when he's in

Brighton. There is still no movement on his football career, but I have a feeling he's getting down to the wire on making a decision of what he'll do.

All in all, Vance has demonstrated that he's fully committed to being a part of my life, both in a co-parent sense and a romantic sense.

And these snogging sessions are only winding me up, then leaving me feeling frustrated and needy after I shut my bedroom door.

Without allowing all of my thoughts and what-ifs to stop me from acting, I take Vance's hand.

"Come to bed," I whisper.

It's not a question, but I can tell that my voice has a slight waver to it.

The air shifts instantly. Where once an easy nighttime atmosphere surrounded us, it is now replaced with sizzling chemistry and sexual tension that has been put at bay for years.

"You're sure?" His voice is gruff, pure sex licking up my spine.

I don't nod. I don't speak. I just fist a handful of T-shirt, send him a meaningful gaze, and walk backward to my bedroom.

My feet don't get three steps in before Vance is lifting me off of them and crushing me to his body. His hands grip me under the arms, where he practically throws me into the air and catches me around the waist. The ease with which he juggles me is erotic and reminds me of the very creative ways we used to make love.

My thighs spread, pressing against the growing bulge in his pants. I might moan, or squeal, but it's swallowed by those harsh lips surrounded by a bristle of beard. Vance is not gentle as he walks me toward my bed, we've both waited too long to be able to contain ourselves. As it is, my hands are yanking at his midnight black hair, my lips consuming his mouth from the vantage point I have above him.

I grip his large, muscled shoulders as we sway, almost drunk on the kisses we're laying siege to each other's mouths.

His hands knead my arse, and with every ministration, I grind farther into his hips. Spread my legs wider. I'm not even naked yet and I can feel that familiar pull of an orgasm low in my belly.

Finally, after what seems like decades but is only milliseconds, we reach the bed. Not even bothering to deposit me, to detach me, Vance just tumbles us both right down onto the mattress, my old queen squeaking with an *oomph*.

"No waking the baby," I whisper-groan, and then he's covering my mouth with that scratchy, insanity-inducing beard.

I wonder what it will feel like between my legs.

He comes up over me, pulling his shirt off with one hand behind his neck like some sort of porn god. I barely get to appreciate it though, because in the next second, he's ripping my flannel shirt clean off, buttons scattering around the room.

Holy fuck. The entire crotch of my knickers floods with wetness.

Vance is not a talkative bloke. And even less so in the bedroom. It's like he's a heat-seeking missile, his only mission is to get me off so bloody well that I scream to the heavens and chant incantations. What energy he conserves from keeping his mouth shut is poured into my body, into his hands and his massive cock and his teeth on my neck.

It's all moving so fast, but then again, we can't seem to move fast enough. We've been moving in this direction for so long, perhaps since the day he left me. Two slow-moving asteroids just biding their time until impact.

And now that we're colliding, we're going to bring the whole world down with us.

My nails scrape down the carved muscles of his abs.

His fingers shove the cups of my bra down, trussing up my breasts until he can bite and lathe my nipples.

I fumble with the tie of his sweatpants, finally getting them loose enough to shove down his hips.

That talented mouth presses open-mouthed kisses up and down my upper body, until I'm squirming with need.

My hand finds his cock, rigid and twitching as I stroke it.

"Vance ..." I moan, twisting my head to the side into a pillow as his fingers dip into my knickers.

He finds me, wet and greedy for him, as I pump my hips in time to the thrust of his digits.

In a matter of seconds, we're both panting and snogging with so much intensity that I almost can't breathe. All of it is stealing my breath; from the way he's working the bundle of nerves between my legs to the sheer insanity that the man about to make me orgasm is none other than one of my greatest dreams and most heart-wrenching nightmares. My heart and lungs almost can't believe it's him, as if the shock of knowing Vance is about to be inside me is causing them to malfunction.

Right as I'm about to spill over the edge, as his prick becomes infinitely harder and hotter on my palm, Vance rips my pants down my legs. I'm not even sure his are fully off, and I'm still trussed up in my bra with my flannel shirt laying limply on my shoulders.

But neither of us can worry about clothing, or whether or not all of it is off. It's a desperate act we're in right now, the need to feel. To release. To sprint closer to the brink of losing our minds together.

With one flit of his hooded chocolate eyes on mine, an understanding that no one is stopping this, Vance pushes all the way into me with one stroke.

And I nearly seize.

The wave of pleasure with a bite of pain crashes over my

body like the most vicious of waves. All I can do is ride it out, give my body over to it and hope to remain intact on the other side.

Gripping Vance's shoulders, I meet his pace, grinding my hips into his each time he smashes back into me. With every backstroke, I suck in air. With every new thrust, I'm powerless to keep the moans inside my throat.

This.

This is what I've been missing all these years.

This is why I've never been able to fall in love with anyone else.

This, some undefinable, inexpressible feeling, is why Vance and I work on a level that blows every other man away.

Before I even realize it's happening, my body begins to shake. Vance never lets me go, the sides of my face held in his hands. He watches as the orgasm pulls me under like a rip current, ravaging every nerve inside me.

"I love you."

Three words. The only ones Vance says the entire time we've had our hands and mouths on each other. The only ones he says while he's inside me.

Uttered just before he buries his face in my hair and cries out sharply, emptying himself into me.

28

VANCE

When I wake up on Christmas morning, it's in Lara's bed.

We're wrapped up in each other, naked save for her underwear between us. All of those petite, willowy limbs threaded through mine. I try to lie perfectly still, petrified I might wake her before I get my fill of properly looking at her. Because, blimey, what a view this is.

It has been so long since I've shared a bed with her, much less was inside of her. Not that the shagging wasn't ... shite, I was a bloody caveman during that first round. With how desperate, animalistic, and silent I was, but, *Christ*, if it wasn't euphoric. We both needed it, to get it out of our systems. I've been manic with the need to just drive into her, and that's what I'd done.

But after ...

We probably should have gone to sleep, what with the four a.m. wake-up call we knew was coming from Mason on Christmas morning. Instead, Lara and I spent the night re-educating ourselves on the other's body. She rode me slow and gentle; I took her from behind while her hands gripped the headboard. When we were both too knackered and spent, but still randy, we laid on our sides and grinded into each other until our climaxes slipped us into a dreamlike state.

And then I woke up, somewhere around five—bless Mason for the late Christmas wake-up—and simply gazed at Lara. It's not often these days that I get to study her in such a peaceful state; she's usually running around with our son or for work or buying house supplies or completing one of the other seventy items on her to-do list. I don't know how she manages it, but she makes it look so easy.

She didn't tell me she loved me back. I said it right before I came the first time, and I meant it. Blimey, I've meant it all these months I've been saying it. I never put words into the world that I don't one hundred percent stand behind, and these are no different. I'm blunt, there is no bullshit when it comes to me.

I'm also not dramatic, or needy. If and when Lara wants to tell me she's in love with me, I'll be here to hear it. In the meantime, I already know she does. The looks she gives me, the way her eyes lock onto mine as I caress her naked body ... that is louder than words.

When she finally woke up, she blinked, gave me a shy, cheeky smile, and then hopped out of bed to get our boy.

I've spent the day with my family, Lara and Mason, and eventually my parents, Harlow, and her mum. It's one of the best days I've had in ... well, forever.

But, I have to head back to the academy tomorrow, which I am not happy about in the slightest.

And in the blink of an eye, I am in a car headed for London.

I got the call two days ago. Remus needs a break, and this match is just a friendly. So, Niles is calling me in. I hung up the phone, sat on my dorm room bed, and almost stared a hole through the cement floor I looked at it for so long.

This is my chance. I know it's a long shot that Remus will leave, or that I'll be named a starter after one match. But this is the only chance I am going to get and I *will* knock their bloody socks off.

"This is your shot, mate. Clean sheet or bust." Kingston jumps up and down, his already wiry energy soaring to new heights.

He's only mirroring my silent sentiments, but per usual, I'm on edge in the locker room. I loathe sitting in here, ruminating on the pressures before a match. I just want to fucking get out there.

"Gee, thanks, mate. Really keeps the pressure off." I roll my eyes.

He swats a hand at me. "You're already feeling pressure. But you're an animal, we all know that. You feed on that shite."

Jude nods in agreement. "This is your moment. Mason here?"

I swallow. "Yes. Lara brought him with her."

It's lucky enough that this match falls during Lara's winter holiday from school, and that made it possible for her to travel to London with Mason. I'm not sure my son quite grasps what I do for a living, but I know he loves football and he'll be chuffed to watch my match. I just hope I can make him proud—not that he'll know it until he's older.

And for Lara to be here, at my London debut? She's never seen me play before. I never let her. I'm so ashamed of what a pompous arse I was back then that it roils in my gut to think about it. Whenever she'd ask when we were dating as teenagers, I'd tell her I didn't want anything to ruin my focus.

What a naïve wanker I was. If anything, I have more adrenaline and laser-sharp focus running through my veins today *because* she's here.

Part of me can't wait to get out onto that pitch and show her why I've made all the sacrifices I have for this game. Part of me can't wait for this match to be over, because I'll have my son and the woman I love waiting for me. Maybe that's why all of these blokes have families. It feels bloody good to know you have something to go home to win or lose.

"Let's go, mates." Jude nods to the locker room, and we all stand at once, marching into the tunnel.

This is it.

29

LARA

When I walk into the Rogue Football Stadium family room, it's full of an assortment of people.

Gorgeous models, who are no doubt the wives and girlfriends of these first class athletes. Older looking couples, some of whom are probably the parents of the players. Blokes who are probably about the same age as me; maybe they're friends of Vance's teammates?

And now, I'm one of them. Well, for today, that is.

"Mummy, candy!" Mason squeals, pointing across the room.

Sure enough, there is a full buffet of food, complete with a dessert bar that boasts jars of colorful candy. *Brilliant*. He'll be asking me for those the entire match.

"Blimey, you look like your dad," the petite blonde sitting next to the most famous model in the world says.

Turning my head their way, from where I noticed them out of the corner of my eye, I smile in a cautious way.

I notice Poppy Raymond right off because who wouldn't? She's graced the pages of every magazine I've read since the age of fifteen. She's even more statuesque and gorgeous in person, and it makes sense that this is the girl who loves Kingston Phillips. The two of them together burn brighter than the sun.

"This is Mason." I smile down at my son, urging him to smile back at the two women.

The blonde gets up and walks over, bending so she's eye level. "I'm Aria. Do you like animals?"

Ah, Aria. I've listened to a song or two, but honestly, don't have much time for anything in my life so I don't recognize her. But the name, I know for sure now that this is Jude's fiancée. She's perky, pretty, and genuine in that girl-next-door way. And apparently, my son is already half in love with her.

He latches onto her hand, looking at her in the eyes where she squats in front of him.

"I wike elephants. Um, zebras. Mingos!" Mason rattles off his favorite animals, ending with his abbreviated version of flamingos.

"Those are my favorite, too! I also like dogs, cats, and well, I love all animals, really." Aria gives Mason a megawatt smile, as if they have their own little shared secret now.

And he's eating it up. "Want get candy?"

Bloody hell, he's asking Jude Davies' fiancée on a date across the family suite.

Aria laughs. "Let's do it."

Poppy Raymond stands and makes her way over to us, tearing her eyes off the glass where she's watching Kingston warm up. I'd like to look down and see if I can watch Vance go through his drills, but Mason is already tearing across the room with Aria, so I have to keep my eye on him.

"Hi, I'm Poppy." She extends a perfectly airbrushed hand, as if she's perpetually on a photo shoot.

I've never been a particularly starstruck or celebrity obsessed person, but my God, looking at this woman is like looking straight at the sun.

"Uh, h-hi, I'm, uh, Lara," I stutter and blush.

She smiles as if she knows she has this effect on people. "If you saw the inside of my soul, you'd be sneering at me."

And now I bark out a laugh. "We may have more in common than I initially realized."

You'd have to be living under a rock if you hadn't heard about the massive scandal rocking the modeling community right now. Poppy is one of more than two or three dozen models who had been sexually abused by a famous photographer. The incidents spanned two decades, and all the abuse was to girls who were minors at the time. Poppy was among the strongest of the voices, and she's even started a nonprofit to help victims of abuse.

She is, in all definitions of the word, incredible.

"Anyone who manages to impress Vance has to be ace. I mean, I've known the guy for over a year and he still won't throw a smile in my direction." Poppy winks at me.

She's way nicer than I thought she'd be. There I go, judging books by their covers again.

"Don't worry, surly is his natural state," I assure her.

"Who, Vance?" Aria holds hands with Mason as they return, both holding a cup full of candy.

"How'd you know?" I smirk.

"Because I love that old grizzly bear. Not like that, you know. Jude would throw a fit. I love Vance like a brother. And I cannot believe how much he looks like his dad. It's uncanny."

"Mummy, candy!" Mason holds his cup up to show me, and I smile down at him.

Great, he'll be up forever tonight with all that sugar. Either that, or he'll crash and be cranky. Good, Vance can take care of him.

"Come on, sit with us. The match is about to start," Aria beckons me, and I follow.

These two have an instant camaraderie about them. Maybe it's because all the men we love found each other before they found us, and we've been inducted into their tribe.

After setting Mason up with his candy, stuffed whale, and a book, I look down onto the field. Sure enough, the opening whistle just sounded, and the Rogue players begin to scatter into formation.

There he is, Vance Morley. Standing broad and formidable in front of the net. He's the anchor of the squad, the one who keeps them grounded and steady, and I can't imagine any other job in the world for him aside from this. The gorgeous, intimidating, brick wall of a man with the laser-focused expression.

Blimey, my heart does a backflip staring at him.

"Come on, Jude," Aria chants under her breath, and a quick glance at Poppy and Aria confirms their eyes are seeking their own men.

The first half goes by in a flash of lightning, with Jude scoring one goal, Kingston scoring the other, and Vance fending off three shots on goal.

Mason is practically asleep in my lap, and Aria gets up to fetch me a sandwich and drink during intermission.

"Is it ... do you love being a mum?" Poppy asks, eyeing Mason where he snoozes against my chest.

I nod, careful not to jostle him. "It's the best and hardest thing I've ever done."

Aria returns with my refreshments before Poppy and I can delve further into the conversation. "Look, they're starting back up."

With Mason asleep, I can turn more of my attention to stalking Vance on the pitch below. He's so calculated in his movements, so precise and skilled in every way when it comes to this game. I see it now, why he's so dedicated. Not only is this game his lifeblood, but the game needs him. He's too brilliant at football for it to let him go.

"Oh my God!" I cry, careful to shush the end of my outburst so as not to wake Mason.

Vance nearly missed a shot on goal by a fingertip's length, but used the extra oomph of his falling body to save it. Bugger, that was close. The match drags but also flies by. It's an odd sensation, feeling like each minute is the length of a year but also checking the game clock and seeing them tick by.

As they reach the end of the ninety-minute mark, I turn to Aria, who is biting on her nails. Rogue has a two goal lead, but anything can happen now.

"I hope there isn't a lot of stoppage time," Poppy remarks.

She doesn't seem as invested in the sport as Aria and I are, gripping the edge of our seats, but I send up a prayer that her wish comes true.

Three minutes flash on the big board on one side of the stadium, and I blow out a breath. I've watched enough of Vance's matches to know that isn't a horrid amount of extra time.

"Come on, mates, just hold this one," Aria mutters under her breath.

I can barely watch, peeping through the hand that's slapped over my eyes. Because while Aria might be cheering on the squad, this rests on Vance's shoulders. The rest of the team has done their job, scoring goals and putting Rogue on top. Vance is the one who has to stop any attempts, who has to guard against goals being scored.

Time ticks down. Two minutes and thirty seconds. Two minutes. One minute and thirty seconds.

Vance bounces on the balls of his feet, shifting back and forth in the net and spreading his hands as if he's ready for anything that might come his way.

Just when I think we're in the clear, that Rogue has won with just twenty seconds left to go, the opposing team lines up with a quick three passes and—

Shoots right toward Vance and the net.

I swear, time stops.

With catlike reflexes, Vance picks a direction and lunges his body in it.

And thankfully, his decision is spot on. The football bounces off of his abs, those beautiful sculpted muscles, and rolls onto the grass in front of him. Players run for it, cleats aimed directly at Vance's face, but he doesn't pay the danger any mind. Pushing off the ground and springing low across his area, he falls on the ball, scooping it to him like a precious baby.

The whistle goes off. The end of the match.

"They won!" I jump up, pulling a grumpy, half-sleeping Mason with me and cheering.

"Mummy," he protests, rubbing his eyes.

I ignore him, kissing his cheek emphatically. "They won the football match, love!"

Today was a big test for Vance, and he passed. It may not mean a thing, but he bloody won, took his team to victory.

"Great win for Vance." Aria comes in to hug me, and Poppy gives me a genuine smile.

We all wait in the family room for the men to come up, and about half an hour later, they do.

"Won the match!" A now wide awake Mason says as Vance comes toward him.

"That we did, chap." He tosses Mason in the air and then rests him on one hip.

I know it's daft, right in front of my child who doesn't yet know this man is his father, but I press up on my toes and plant a kiss on Vance's lips. It may be the three-piece, charcoal gray suit he's donned, or the way the ink-black tie around his neck matches his eyes.

"Way to go, keeper."

He smirks. "Could get used to that post-match ritual."

"You lot want to come to over for a pint?" Jude asks, and I sense he may be warming up to me.

Not that I've had much more contact with his mates after Vance brought them to the pub by my school, but I have a feeling what Aria says goes. And she seems to like Mason and me, so Jude will have to like us, too.

"Little mate, good to meet you." Kingston bends down, extending his fist to Mason for him to bump it.

Instantly, my son does, thinking it's hilarious. Well, I guess that Kingston Phillips charm works on both genders.

"I'm a little knackered," I say, the adrenaline leaving my bones and leaving the need for a good rest.

It's been a long match, and I'm spent.

"We'll go back to the hotel, maybe catch you a little later." Vance's voice says there is no questioning this decision.

Neither Jude nor Kingston push him on it, and I realize this is how the dynamic in their group works. They know Vance very well.

Vance slings an arm around my shoulder, with Mason still in his arms, and steers us through the maze-like hallways of the building.

The second we push out of the rear exit doors, the onslaught begins.

"*Vance, have you been paying child support?*"

"*What does your ex think of your dates with Poppy Raymond's friend?*"

"*Who has sole custody?*"

"*Can we get DNA test results?*"

"*What does your ex-fiancé think of you spending time in London with Vance Morley?*"

By the time we get through the crowd, my hands are

clamped around Mason's ears and he's half-buried in my coat. That was like walking through a minefield, with bombs detonating every time we took a step. My skin seems to be singed and scratched, my heart torn to pieces by the shrapnel of ugly, *ugly* words.

Vance is practically shaking me as we get into the back of the limo. "Lara, are you okay? *Lara*?"

I blink, because I can't speak right now or I'll cry. When Mason pulls his head up, I attempt a smile but it feels wonky.

"I wasn't prepared ..." I trail off, because the shock of it is still pulsing in my system.

"I know. I'm sorry. I'm sorry," he chants, crushing both of us to his chest.

We stay like that, a little unit, as the car races through the streets of London. Those people, they were so full of spite. They don't even know us, have no idea the nature of our co-parenting, romantic relationship, the vulnerability of our son ... and yet, they seem to think it's their business. Why is the world the way it is?

"I set up a high tea reservation ... we don't have to go, though. I know it's not great timing, that was rough." Vance's eyes are dark and hard as flint as he pulls back.

And in the midst of all this, he set up a date for us. Vance Morley, the most unromantic man I've ever met, took the time to set up a date for me. In London of all places.

What *is* this world?

"I think, I mean." I shake my head, trying to clear the funk those paparazzi planted in there. "Who will watch Mason?"

"Actually, I already asked Aria. She's waiting at the hotel now. I wanted to surprise you."

On one hand, I didn't think I could even let Mason out of my arms now. All I want to do is shelter him from every vile thing in the world, to erase all the rubbish being said about his parents. About his biology.

On the other, here is the man I've been asking to prove himself to me, proving himself to me. Vance did not do hearts and flowers, yet here he is doing it. I shouldn't take that lightly.

My head is such a mess of confusion, I don't even know if I can make a choice.

"We don't have to go." Vance waves it off, but I can feel the defeat in his voice.

I'm the one who chose to keep Mason from him. And yet, he's never once told the media that. He's just taken their attacks, and I have a feeling their barbs are worse than he's ever let on to me.

"No, let's do it. We're in London. Together. I want to have tea."

An hour later—after we've gotten Mason settled with Aria and I've given her all of the important information and numbers, and subsequently gone mental having to leave my child with a person who's never watched him before—Vance pulls out my chair in the poshest tea room I've ever seen.

The wallpaper is floral and beautiful; the chairs tufted with gold accents, and all the china on the table is real and dainty.

"Vance, this is lovely," I tell him because it is.

"I'm glad you like it."

Blimey, is that a blush? Is Vance Morley, the iron giant, happily embarrassed? It's almost too adorable for words.

The server brings the two pots of tea we ordered to try, and a spiraling sandwich tray that belongs in a five-star restaurant, in front of me.

"So, this is London." I chuckle.

I've been once or twice with Mum, but barely remember those visits now. No, I've always been a Brighton girl, the kind who is more comfortable in beachside eateries and flip-flops than high heels and chic nightclubs.

"The one and only. So, did you enjoy the match?" he asks.

I realize we haven't even spoken about it since my only congratulations in the family suite. Ah, to be a parent. Forgetting half of the things you're supposed to think about to focus on your child.

Humbling myself, because football has always been a hotbed issue between us, I take a deep breath.

"I see now why you dedicate so much time to the sport. You're not just a natural, Vance. I could tell, even from up in that suite, that you love it. The rush, the precision, you're so … I'm not sure I can find a word. This game is your calling."

Intense mocha eyes assess me. "I used to think that. Now, I'm not so sure."

He pours me some tea out of the pot; the steam billowing over the sides of the cream-colored floral teacup. Then, Vance selects a sandwich, because apparently doubt doesn't steal a man's ability to eat. Nothing seems to steal a man's ability to eat.

"You were brilliant out there. I know I haven't been supportive in the past of football, maybe I've tainted it in your eyes in that way. But, you should have seen Mason, Vance. He was so excited, so proud of you. The fact that you have known what you wanted to do since you were his age, and you're actually achieving it, it's magnificent."

The usually self-assured, stoic, ridiculously attractive man sitting across from me has a look on his face like I've just said the exact right thing he needed to hear.

His large, dexterous fingers find my leg, massaging the fabric just over my knee. Instantly, a flush runs through me.

"Enough about football. Try your tea," Vance urges.

I take a sip of tea and then feel his hand moving up my thigh. The path of heat that radiates from his palm into my jeans is scintillating. The cool mint of the tea mixed with the temperature of it in my mouth, and his hand grazing up my leg, touching my hip ...

Oh, so *this* is why he brought me to tea. Not that I care, it's been almost four days since I woke up to him in my bed Christmas morning, and I haven't been able to calm the raging storm of lust inside me since.

"Do you want to meet me in the bathroom?" Vance's eyebrow raises a fraction, and I know that for him, this is the epitome of flirting.

"Yes," I answer, almost breathless.

Who knew that when I agreed to a night in London, it would end in high tea and a bathroom shagging?

30

LARA

"And his nappies are in here, he likes to sleep with the green blanket, not the blue—"

"Love, they've got this." Vance's gentle voice and touch at my elbow interrupt the minor breakdown I'm having.

Roberta and Clive Morley regard me with patient smiles, and to be fair I shouldn't even be grilling these kind people. They've only known about their grandson for a short while, and in that time, have come to love and cherish him like the light of their world. Roberta dotes on him hand and foot, sewing him blankets and stocking his favorite snacks. Kip sneaks him cookies before dinner and has taught him everything there is to know about rugby, much to Vance's chagrin.

Mason's new grandparents love him so much it's almost tangible, and I'm the one who kept them from doing so for so long. I should be thanking them on my knees for being so forgiving, and for not putting up more of an argument when I did eventually allow them to meet Mason.

"Lara, he's going to be spoiled rotten. Do not worry. We'll still brush his teeth and feed him vegetables, but he'll know more love this weekend than there might be in the entire world. Have fun. Take a few days off. You kids deserve it."

Roberta palms my cheek in a motherly way, and smiles fondly at Vance.

This will be the first time I've ever been away from Mason for more than a night, and I am going mental.

When Vance proposed we get away for the short break he has, I couldn't refuse. Three days with no one but Vance to get more acquainted than we already are? Count me in.

But really, I'm going for the all-expenses paid drinks and massage I was promised. Vance, who I now refer to as the king of wooing, planned the entire trip to the Canary Islands with the sole purpose of lavishing me in relaxation. When I asked why, he told me I'd been in the trenches with Mason since the beginning, and I deserved a good vacation. *Swoon*.

"Okay, then, I guess this is it, love." I bend to my son, who has been ignoring all of us in favor of his Buzz Lightyear action figure.

"Bye-bye, Mummy," he says in that sweet little voice of his as he leans in to let me kiss his forehead.

Vance bends down beside me. "Be good for Pa and Nana, all right? Love you, Super Boy."

"Luf you, Daddy," Mason chirps, taking us all by surprise.

Vance is so still, I think he might keel over of a heart attack or something. I hear him sniffle, and then wipe a tear from his eye, before scooping Mason up into a hug. Above us, Roberta is most definitely sobbing, and I can't help the contented few tears I shed.

And, I guess the moral of the story is, don't complicate things. Children are pretty intuitive. Eventually, I suppose, Mason just figured out on his own that Vance is his father.

Out of all the pain and heartbreak that we've had to endure, this moment is worth it.

"If you don't get your arse in this water, I'm going to drag you in."

I take back everything I said before. I like Vacation Vance the best. He's freer, not so stern and actually laughed at a joke one of the swim-up pool bartenders made today.

"Oh, I'd like to see you try," I taunt him, running up our private sandy beach.

The villa he booked for us on an exclusive resort in the Canary Islands is ... blimey, it's magnificent. You know those commercials you see, or maybe your wildest dreams, when there is a couple all alone on some white sand beach? And you think, hmm, wouldn't it be brilliant if they could just run around naked all day?

We could. Vance and I could do that. On our private beach, with our private villa, and private ocean.

The house—yes it's not a room for vacation, it's an actual house bigger than my flat in Brighton—is luxurious and gleaming with its ocean-side decor, four-poster king bed and soaking tub that overlooks the vast aquamarine ocean. We can choose to stay in our villa or join the other vacationers on the resort at the four swim-up bars, three Michelin star restaurant, or in the world-renowned spa.

I swear, I've died and gone to heaven. Do other people actually live like this? It's a hell of a long way from frigid Brighton and teaching hormone-crazed secondary school students.

"Woman, don't test me."

The next scene is something out of a movie, a very illicit one with an R rating.

Vance emerges from the ocean, water sluicing down every indent of his brawny chest and carved biceps. The dark trail of hair that runs from his navel and disappears down into the black board shorts he wears teases me from the distance. Running one very-talented hand through his midnight black hair as his thighs strain against the fabric of his bathing suit ... blimey, I have to audibly swallow my mouth is so dry.

He eats up the distance between us, and in an instant, I'm thrown over his shoulder.

"I wasn't kidding," he retorts, smug as I beat against the globes of his arse from my upside-down position.

"Vance! Put me down! This isn't funny!" Even though I cackle as he swats my bikini-clad arse.

From what I can see in this precarious state, our venue has changed. We were outside, enjoying the endless sunshine and margaritas in the cooler a butler had brought us. Now, I spot the marble tiled floor of our villa, and the chunky beige rug of the bedroom it boasts.

"Oh, I know it's not funny." The growl that emits from his throat as he slides me down his body and onto the bed is carnal.

I've been under him on this bed more times than I count on this vacation, and we've only been here for two days. We've shagged standing, sitting, lying, and probably every other position known to man. Like I said, there is just something about Vance and me. This inability to keep our hands off each other for very long when we occupy the same space.

As he lowers his head to my breasts, my nipples are already hard as bullets for him.

But he bypasses them, instead skating his teeth up my collarbone and over to my shoulder, where he grunts as his mouth makes contact with the strap of my bikini. And pulls. The scraps of fabric pool around my breasts.

Bloody hell, the man is a lustful maniac. He's just untied me with nothing but his teeth.

Lazily, I explore his bare chest with my hands, my movements languid as Vance stokes the fire inside me higher and higher. He's stripped me by the time my fingers dip beneath the waistband of his trunks, and push until I can feel the warm, smooth flesh of his ass. I sink my nails into it until Vance curses, and my inner she-devil smirks with satisfaction. I love affecting this usually stoic man.

Before I realize what he's doing, those broad shoulders are halfway down my body, hovering over me until I feel Vance's breath right between my thighs.

"Oh my ..." A wail careens out of me as his tongue dips into my center.

In seconds, I'm bucking like a prize-winning bull as Vance keeps his steely grip on my hips, his tongue doing magical, wonderful things to me. My fists pull at the sheets, at his hair, scratching his arms.

Vance was always *very* skilled at this particular portion of foreplay, it was like he could read my mind while down between my legs. The familiar pull of my orgasm threatens to consume me, but just as I'm about to tip over the edge, he stops.

Crawling back up the Egyptian-cotton sheets, Vance plants open mouth kisses on my lips as he lines us up.

Vance slides into me, my core already dripping wet, and skims one hand down my right arm until our hands are clasped. I pant as he moves my arm, planting it above my head and pinning my fingers to the pillows beneath. He repeats the motion with my other arm, and then he's poised above me like some primed tiger looking down at his prey.

With long, deep, slow strokes, he begins to assault my senses, my nerves, and every pore on my body in the best way possible. I can't take my eyes off him, and when he looks down to see where we're joined, I look too.

It's erotic as all hell.

I love him, we both know I do. I just can't say it. I'm terrified.

Terrified that Vance will take those words, and walk away from me with them in his back pocket again.

As much as I can, I try to relay my feelings with my eyes. They're boring into him right now, each of us nearly breathless as he thrusts in hard, slow motions. One more and I'll ...

My body erupts at the exact moment Vance lets out a shouting growl, and his hands force mine farther down into the mattress. We come together, taking and giving pleasure equally.

Hours later, I wake to the sunset pouring through the windows of the room, basking Vance and me in stripes of butter yellow and coral pink. He's softly breathing, his head nestled on my chest and one of my legs thrown over his waist.

This is perfection, in the purest form.

There are so many things we have to get back to. Parenting, jobs, frustrations of the real world.

For as long as we can keep those things out, shut the door of our villa and live our lives to make love ...

I'll do it.

31

VANCE

Being in my dorm room feels like being in prison.

I'm locked away, alone. Lara and Mason aren't here. Jude and Kingston aren't here. It's bloody cold on this campus, and in here with the draft from the old stained-glass windows that were only ever meant to be used in a church setting.

Just a week ago, I was on a beach with a naked Lara, sinking my cock into her while the ocean wind blew at our backs. I want to be back there, in paradise with the mother of my child.

We've shagged more time than I can count in the last month, since that first time on Christmas Eve. Making up for lost time, I say. Lara berates me every day with how sore she is, but I know it's half-joking complaints. She's the one who jumps my bones each time I walk through her flat door when I get back to Brighton.

And now I'm here, in this bloody purgatory, awaiting my fate. I do what I've always done. Go to training sessions. Hit the weight room. Attend games. Eat in the dining hall. I'm so fucking sick of this life that I question why I'm here every minute of every day.

As if her ears were ringing, my mobile begins to do the same, the screen lighting up with Lara's name.

"Hi," I sigh into the phone, needing to hear her voice.

Now that we're solid again, or as solid as we can be for now, I find more and more that I need her to feel settled. If I'm not with her, if I go even an hour without communicating with her, something inside my chest goes haywire.

How had I survived those years without her? Perhaps it's why I'd been so damn moody for the majority of my twenties thus far.

"Hey, love. What are you doing?" I just imagine her cuddled on the couch right now, and I miss her even more than I did before.

"Sitting in this godforsaken dorm room," I grumble. "How was your day? How is Mason?"

Lara huffs out a breath. "Well, I had two students go to the headmaster's office for mobile use during class. But I did get that lesson plan passed on *The Scarlet Letter*, the one I told you about. So a win and a loss. Mason was splendid today, ate dinner in ten minutes flat. It was a rare, but great, night."

At least he cooperated for her tonight. I feel so much guilt being away from them, not being able to help in my half of the parenting duties.

"Good. I miss you both."

"I know, we miss you, too. Mason keeps rambling about Daddy. It's so cute." Her voice warms.

"I hate being here." My melancholy continues to deepen, and I feel like a sulking teenager, but I can't help it.

"You won't be there much longer." Lara tries to put a positive note in her voice.

"You don't know that," I argue, sounding even more dramatic.

"But you played so well in that match Mason and I went to," she argues.

"Nothing has happened as a result of it. I'm sick of being here. I'm sick of working my arse off for nothing."

"So come home to us." Her words are simple, as if they're facts and not suggestions.

"It's not that easy," I snap.

I knew she wouldn't understand. She never did like this as my career.

"I know it isn't." Her voice is just as strained.

It's the age-old problem between us.

"I think we're just both fed up, tired, and missing each other," Lara admits with a sigh.

She's not wrong. This back and forth, trying to live our lives long distance and waiting for some kind of decision to be made about my football future, I feel like it's damaging us. Not so it's visible, but over time the cracks will appear. Just like they did last time. We have a son to think about, and I want to marry Lara, not that she knows it yet. The woman can't even utter the three words I've already said to her out of the fear I'll break her heart again. And who am I to convince her I won't? I'm a child trying to play an adult's game; I can't be a father when I live two hours away, chasing a dream that isn't even at my fingertips.

Hell, being the keeper of RFC isn't even within an arm's length.

"I'll see you this weekend, yeah?" Lara breaks the awkward silence.

I bury my head in my hands, thankful she can't see how defeated I look. "Yeah."

This wasn't how I thought this call would go at all.

"All right."

"Give Mason my love," I tell her.

Lara rings off before I can tell her I love her, too. Probably on purpose, so she wouldn't have to say it back.

And my mood only dips further into gloom. I can't be there for her. I can't be there for Mason. I'm stuck here, trading my loyalty to a club that wants to do nothing but stick me on a shelf.

I'm almost at my breaking point. When I do, I wonder if I'll abandon the dream I've worked my entire life to achieve.

32

LARA

"Mum! Mum!"

I rush into the emergency room of the Brighton Hospital, my eyes full of tears and my head spinning like I've been on a carnival ride for hours.

That's how I feel, actually. Sick to my stomach, disoriented, and not sure which way is up.

"Lara? Over here!" She runs at me, and I catch her as we meet in the middle of the dingy, fluorescent-lit hospital hallway.

"A motorbike, it just hopped the curb, I didn't even see it, I didn't ..." Mum's voice is frantic and my heart threatens to burst out of my throat.

"Where is he? *Where is he*?" I'm frantic.

"Are you Mason Logan's mother?" Someone in a white coat comes up to me.

I assume he's a doctor, because why would he be asking and look like that. "Yes. Yes, that's me."

"Good, we've been waiting to give a guardian his prognosis."

"Is he okay?" I choke out, not able to stomach that I'm saying these words.

The doctor's face splits into a small, reassuring smile, and instantly some of the waves of nausea wracking my body dissipate.

"Your son is going to be just fine. He was lucky, or maybe he just has a tough skull. Nothing but a few scrapes and bruises, one that he needed a couple stitches for. Other than a broken arm, that will heal fully in six to eight weeks, he's healthy as a horse. Good genes this lad has. He's lucky he doesn't have a concussion or any other internal injuries. He's just fine, Ms. Logan."

A breath, one that's been caught in my lungs since my mother called me screaming just half an hour ago, whooshes from my chest. I bend over, releasing a few sobs, and then straighten to wipe my eyes.

"Thank you. *Thank you.*" I can't seem to say anything else.

When I got the call from Mum, where she stood on the side of Main Street as an ambulance loaded Mason inside, I instantly dropped the paperwork I'd stayed after school to complete. Her voice had been so panicked, I thought the sky was falling. It was, my sky that is. The boy who hangs the moon for me had been mowed down by a reckless motorcyclist.

"Can I see him?" I ask, my voice fraught with need and exhaustion.

"Right this way." The doctor motions, and I follow.

When I barge into Mason's room, not bothering to shield my still-present panic before I see my son, I'm shocked to see who is standing beside him.

"Louis, what are you doing here?" My eyes roam over my ex-fiancé before falling to my son.

Mason looks so small and delicate in the bed, the adult mattress swallowing his almost two-year-old frame. He has a bandage around his head, a cast on his arm, but his eyes look clear and he's smiling at something Louis must have just said.

Rushing to him, I try to gingerly gather him in my arms. "Oh, my baby."

Silent tears fall down my cheeks, ones my son can't see because I've hugged him so close.

"Look, Mummy, green!" He lifts his right arm, which I now know from his doctor is broken in two places.

The cast they've put on him is lime green, and he looks thrilled that he gets to wear it. I hope he keeps that attitude for the next six weeks.

"Wow, buddy, that looks brilliant! Can I sign it?" I ask him, putting on my best Mummy voice.

"Louis, sign!" My son flashes a megawatt smile at the man who used to tuck him into bed.

"They called me as I was the second emergency contact," Louis explains, looking awkward and uncomfortable.

Shite, I really needed to update the medical information on file for Mason.

"Thank you for coming." It's an automatic response, because I'm grateful that he came when some nurse called about a boy who isn't technically his son.

"I'd do anything for him." He nods.

We fall silent, and after kissing Mason a few more times, I step back so that he and Louis can briefly chat. It's clear that my ex can't stay, but he did come in Mason's time of need, and for that, I can allow him to say a few words to the boy he raised from infancy.

"It was ... good to see you, Lara." Louis makes a move like he might hug me.

My opinion of him changed that night he showed up drunk to my flat, and though we haven't spoken, I realize I still am not over what he said about Vance.

So I step back, waving a hand. "Thank you for being here for Mason."

Louis goes with a regretful glance back at us.

I cuddle up in Mason's bed with my body spooning his. I'm not sure why the universe ever allows children to experience pain or hurt. If I could, I'd take every blow lined up against him and then some. As a mother, I should have the option to sub myself in for the bad things that will happen to him.

We stay this way until he falls asleep, his soft breathing blowing through the material of my sweater.

When my mobile begins to ring in my pocket, I extract myself carefully from my son and move to the opposite side of the room.

Vance doesn't even bother to say hello when I pick up.

"What the hell is going on, Lara?" Vance demands on the other end of the phone.

After everything I've been through today, his berating of me is the last thing I need. I've been so wrapped up in getting to the hospital, making sure Mason is okay, and conferring with doctors that I forgot to update Vance.

Immediately, my claws come out. "Why are you asking like that? Piss off, it's been the worst afternoon over here and I don't need shite from you."

What kind of poison was in his tea today? We've been on very good terms, *splendid* terms in fact, and he's going to come at me guns blazing while our son lies in a hospital bed? Aside from that phone call yesterday. The one where we hung up without saying how much we cared about each other, and another crack splinters in the surface of our relationship we thought was smooth.

"I just got a call from some local Brighton pissant reporter wanting a comment on his story. Said it was about my son being involved in an accident, and me not being there to care for him. Called me a deadbeat dad. What the hell happened? Is Mason all right?"

That motherfucker. That complete and utter bastard, bloody wanker!

I'm going to murder Louis. Clearly, after I politely banished him from Mason's room, he'd gone to get his bitter rocks off. With the media.

"That git," I mutter, though Vance has no idea what I'm talking about. "I'll deal with the papers, I know who it was. I'm sorry, I'm sorry. It all happened so suddenly, he was out on Main Street with my mum when a motorbike jumped the sidewalk and hit him. He's fine, though, all things considered. Bumps, a couple of stitches, and a broken arm that will heal. He's so excited about the cast, I think he barely notices the pain."

"What? He was hit by a motorbike. Bloody hell. My God." Vance sounds so worried and shocked, I'm sure it isn't easy to get news like this when he can't be with Mason in the same room.

"He's okay, love. Really. One of the nurses promised him ice cream and now that's all he's fixated on."

"I'll hop in the car now. I'll be there in two hours," Vance says hurriedly, and I think I hear him throwing things into a bag.

"Are you sure? Don't you have a match this weekend?" Of course, I want him here, but I don't want him to think I'm pulling him away from anything.

"Fuck the match. I'm coming to hold my son." His voice is full of concern.

"Call me when you get close, I'll let you know if we've left the hospital yet. Drive safe, Vance, I don't need the other most important man in my life hurt, too."

"Tell Mason I'll be there soon. I love him. I love you."

And because I still can't bloody get over myself, I say, "We'll be waiting for you."

33

LARA

I find Louis sitting on a bench outside.

Though my child is lying in a hospital bed upstairs, no matter that my mother is with him, I know I need to do this. I need to, once and for all, put closure on this relationship. Louis and I never settled the hurt between us, and apparently it allowed him to take it and turn it into rage. Against the person I love most.

"You're a fucking wanker, you know that?" My introduction is anything but kind.

Louis's head snaps up, and his eyes are red-rimmed. Like he's been crying. Or maybe he's drunk. Either way, my hands ball into fists.

"I let you stay by his bedside, let you near him to comfort him. And then what do you do? You go outside and give a statement to some bloody reporter about *my* family. I know you're hurt, and I'm to blame for what happened between us, but don't you dare take that out on Mason. Ever."

My voice is so cutting, I'm surprised there isn't a knife to Louis's throat. But that's what he gets for putting my baby in harm's way.

"Lara, I shouldn't have said those things." He sighs, his hand raking through his hair.

"You think? Do you know the damage you've caused? Imagine if Mason saw one of those headlines later in life. Or if some arsehole kid at nursery school whose parents loathe me said something to him? That's his father, Louis, whether you like it or not. And Vance has done a wonderful job of showing up. He can't help it that his job keeps him away on certain days. Not that it's any of your business, but he's been around loads more than you have. When I called off our engagement, you promised that wouldn't be the end of your relationship with Mason. But apparently, that's exactly what happened."

"It's just been hard for me. Everything was taken from me," he complains.

I'm tough because I have to be, but I still have a soul. I know what I did to Louis isn't fair, to be honest it was pure shite. He had every reason to feel sorrow, to not want to come around me and my new beau.

Pulling back on the pit bull inside my chest, I make my tone softer. "I'm sure it's awkward to come visit. Lord knows I am so very sorry, Louis. I didn't do right by you. I can't imagine the hurt you're going through, and I wish I could fix that. But that doesn't give you the liberty to trash us to the tabloids. Do you know the shite we're going to have to endure now? Even if it's retracted, that stain will follow Vance around."

"I never meant to hurt Mason." A sob escapes his throat, and I pat him awkwardly on the shoulder.

At one time, I thought I loved this man. But, after being with Vance, I see it was only friendship. Companionship. I never felt the intense, all-consuming, frustrating, heartbreaking love I do for the father of my child. But Louis was there for me in a time when I could lean on no one else. I'll never forget that.

"I know you didn't. And he still loves you very much. I will never keep you from being a part of his life."

Louis glances up, his brown eyes catching mine. "Thank you. I know I need to do better."

"You were always the better one of us. But if you ever talk to a reporter again, I'll come for you. You know I'm a mother lion when it comes to my son, so don't mess with him."

My ex-fiancé nods emphatically because he has to feel more rotten inside than I feel pissed at him.

Maybe this was the closure we needed, because something in me felt unsettled up until this point. For so long, I've felt horrible about what I did to Louis. Kissing Vance when I was still with him, breaking off our engagement, making it uncomfortable for him to see the boy he'd raised since I gave birth.

With that guilt sitting on my heart, I hadn't been able to move forward. I didn't love Louis, but I also felt truly awful about the wrong I'd done him. Mix that with the frustration I felt at him for judging that Vance was Mason's father, and now this media slip-up ...

It was a recipe for disaster.

But now, it seems we've corrected it.

And without that pressure on the organ in my chest, the one that only ever belonged to one man, I am free to give it away.

34

VANCE

Mason's dark, thick head of hair rests on my chest, and I can tell by how his chin droops that he's asleep.

My fingers trail up and down his small arm, the one that isn't in the cast, just appreciating this small but oh so important moment. I've been in Brighton for two days, completely ignoring all football responsibilities in favor of spending time mending my son.

Lara walks around the couch and smiles at the sight of us. Pulling out her phone, she aims the camera at us and begins taking photos. I know there must be about twenty-seven of them, because she can never take just one.

"He's down for the count." She pushes a lock of Mason's hair off his forehead as she sits down next to me.

Nuzzling my own head into her shoulder, I nod. "Yes, he is. Brave boy, he's taking a broken better than I ever have."

"You broke a bone?" She sounds surprised.

I forget we weren't together at the time. "About two years before you and I got together. Well, for the first time that is. I broke my collarbone, it hurt like bloody hell for months. I was such a baby about it, Jude and Kingston weren't sympathetic nurses, to say the least."

Lara begins to massage my temples lightly with her fingers, and I don't realize I need the stress relief until she starts doing that.

I've tried to keep my own personal issues tucked away while I've been here. Lara doesn't need my shite on top of everything she's dealing with on the Mason front. If I was scared out of my mind when I found out what happened, she must have been nearly catatonic. I bloody loathe that I wasn't there to hold her hand in the hospital.

But things at Rogue have gotten so dismal that I don't even feel any sense of shame for missing this weekend's academy match. Before Mason, before I realized Lara made me complete, I would have played on a broken leg or if my vision was temporarily disabled. I would have gone out onto that pitch, for that team, even if the coaches had told us there would be snipers firing at us at random. My loyalty has never wavered, until now. Because after a while, when the respect you're giving isn't given in return, you stop making such an effort.

And that only causes more stress. Because I'm not the type of person who gives up or stops giving one hundred percent. I feel like shite that I can't achieve my dream because the club is holding me back, and I also feel like shite because it makes me want to fight against my natural instinct to push myself to the physical and mental limits for my goals.

"Can we go to bed? I want to hold you," I tell her.

Because right now, that's all I want to do. I just want to hold on to the person who means the most to me in the entire world. When I got that call from the reporter about Mason's accident, I was in such a frenzied panic that everything felt unhinged. It felt like my universe was fleeting, like it was sand falling through the cracks of my fingers and I couldn't hold onto it fast enough to make the loss stop.

"Blimey, that sounds fantastic." Lara takes my hand, threading her fingers through mine. "Let's get him into his crib and then mattress here we come."

We make quick work of it, having established a bedtime routine when I'm in town. I take off his clothes from the day, take off his wet diaper and wipe him clean. Then we switch; Lara puts on a new diaper and gets him in pajamas while I close the curtains, get his stuffed whale and turn his night-light on. It's a well-oiled machine now, and a ritual I look forward to.

I shuck off my clothing as Lara goes into the loo attached to her bedroom. Folding down the sheets the way she likes them, I sink into the pillows with a sigh as I wait for her to join me. When she does, in nothing but underwear and a black sleep shirt, her skin smells like the citrusy lotion she rubs into her face each night.

It's all very domestic and settled and I love it. I never realized this was the life I wanted until it was sprung upon me. Now, I can't figure out how to cast aside my dreams to get to this point of the day fast enough.

"Hi," she breathes, moving into my arms that I open to her.

A candle flickers on the dresser across the room, but the vibe between us is not sexual. We're tired, have been running ourselves ragged. No, this is more about companionship tonight. About comfort and relaxation.

"How are you handling all of this?" I haven't checked in with her in a while.

Lara blinks. "I'm fine."

"When a woman says she's fine, she's about ten seconds away from murdering a bloke." I chuckle.

She rolls her eyes. "That's a thing men say to make us sound crazy."

I don't touch that one with a ten-foot pole. I like my bollocks, I'll keep them where they are.

"But really, are you doing okay? Do you need me here more? Do you need more help? I can hire someone, you're not in this alone anymore. And no, I don't mean taking care of you as a baby daddy or some bullshit child support. I mean that I'm in this family now. That I want to take care of you as a man who loves you. Who loves our son."

Her eyes, with irises the color of the ocean we grew up on, seem to melt.

"I know you want to take care of us. But I mean it, Vance, we're really doing well. Of course, I wish you were here all the time, but when you're not, we're okay. I'm tired, yes, but that's motherhood. Your parents have been a big help, my mum is stepping up. We're going to make this work. I want you to take care of us, but I want to take care of you, too. And that means supporting you while you chase your dreams. We can wait for a while."

She sounds more confident than she ever has before about my career. Lara tips her head up, pressing her lips against mine. The kiss is gentle, warm, lazy, and melts half the bones in my body. Her mouth, the one I've dreamed of a thousand nights when we were apart, seems to fit mine and only mine.

But it always nagged me, flicked at the back of my brain. The reason we'd fallen apart in the first place was because I was selfishly pursuing my goals, and Lara didn't want to be the kind of woman who took a back seat to an athlete's life.

I could make a decision soon, or I could get called up suddenly. What would happen if I began to start on the first squad in London? Or worse, what if I'm sold to a club across the world?

Yes, we're making this work. The question is, for how much longer?

35

VANCE

"Remus left for Italia FC."

Kingston shouts into the phone, and I take it away from my ear both over the noise and to check the name on the call.

"Why are you calling me from Jude's mobile?" I ask.

Jude's voice comes through. "He's not. It's me, this git just spoiled the news by jumping the gun and over-shouting me."

I roll my eyes because that's such typical Kingston. "So, what is going on?"

"Have you not read any article or turned on the telly? Are you living under an igloo?" Kingston's voice is incredulous.

"That's not helping, King," I grit out.

Jude clears his throat. "Remus got a better offer from Italia FC this morning. He's been dating that Italian model for some time, and they win the league every year. There had been rumblings of a rift between him and Niles, and now, well, he's gone. Rogue FC needs a keeper. You know what that means."

My heart lurches in my chest at the same time the back of my neck goes slick with nervous sweat. Blimey, this is it. Everything I've worked for, everything I've sacrificed years of my life for, it's all going to come to fruition.

At the same exact moment I think about all of my football dreams coming true, my mind flits over to the dreams that have already come true in my personal life. I promised Lara that I wanted to be there for them, to make this work. And now, at the first sign of Rogue coming to call, I was ready to up and move to London.

She was going to be furious. Maybe. If I can present this to her in a way that makes sense, that enriches our family and can set a good example for Mason then maybe she'll go for it.

There's also the issue of the thoughts I've been having about going to the Brighton FC manager. The idea dawned on me as I drove to the hospital to see Mason after the accident. If I can play in my hometown, and practice down the road from my family, I can be with them all the time. A keeper of my caliber? Sure, Rogue doesn't need me but a lesser team in the league would jump at the shot.

Yes, it takes me closer to home, and they are a fair club. But Rogue is my dream. It's the institution I've put my blood, sweat, and tears into.

This is my chance.

"Have you heard anything?" I ask my two best mates.

"Nothing yet. Word is all the executives are in closed meetings this morning. But we're going to push as hard as we can for you, mate." Kingston has that lion-like protectiveness in his tone.

"It's yours, Vance. We're all going to be together on the pitch again." Jude sounds as if he's nodding, like his master plan is falling into place.

"All right, I have to run. I'm in Brighton and only have limited time with Mason. But if you hear anything, send me a message," I tell them.

We ring off, and I put it out of my mind. The last thing I want to do when I'm with Mason and Lara is focus on work, and I'm only in Brighton for the next thirty-six hours.

I walk back into the flat, the one I've come to think of as home. Lara is sitting cross-legged on the carpet, helping Mason put together a puzzle that, when completed, will show him Old MacDonald's farm. They're so intent, sitting there staring at the pieces as she tries to teach our son patience and problem solving.

How am I supposed to tell her I may be leaving for London? Because when I do, I won't have as lax a schedule as I do now. I'm not a student anymore, so classes and homework don't apply that's why the academy professors and headmasters have been giving me a pass when I leave every couple of days to come home to Brighton.

But if I'm called up to London, I don't know when I'll be able to see them next. My international travel will be increased, the media I'll have to do will skyrocket.

Why in the world is Niles Harrington calling me?

My mobile buzzes in my hand once more. Bloody hell, the manager for Rogue Football Club is calling *me*.

I step outside, back the way I came, to take the call.

The moment feels surreal, as I've waited a long time for this call. Will it be the one I've hoped for or the one I've dreaded? Knowing the situation about what happened this morning with Remus, I'm hoping it's the former. Because they could go in a completely different direction than me.

"Hello, Vance Morley speaking." I have no idea why I decide to make my greeting so formal, and I sound like a wanker.

I try to keep my body from cringing with embarrassment.

"Well, Morley, we have an opening, and we want you to come and compete for the spot," Niles says, my ear pressed against the receiver of my mobile.

And if it's possible, my heart both sinks and soars at the same time. I've been waiting fifteen years to hear that Rogue Football Club wants me to come to London and play for them.

But compete? No. Fuck no. I've busted my arse for those same fifteen years, waiting for it to be my time. They've told me to have patience, that my day in the sun, or in the net depending on who you talk to, would come. Now, it's being offered, but at a cheapened price.

Inside, the rage begins to spread through my veins, and I know I have to tamp it down, keep it under control. It figures that when my moment came, it wouldn't be with a bloody parade or complete jubilation, like Jude's or Kingston's promotions. No, everything always has to be the hard way for me.

"Thank you, sir." I'm diplomatic, not allowing any emotion, good or bad, to sway my tone. "I'll be competing for the starting spot?"

There is clanking in the background, and I can tell that Niles is only half paying attention to me. Which only serves to grate on my nerves more.

"What? Oh, yes, we're bringing in two other keepers to audition, though we favor you since you've been with the club since boyhood. I'll see you when you get to London."

And with that, he's gone.

That phone call should have been one of the best of my life, and as I ring off, I'm left feeling exasperated and annoyed. There is no sense of massive accomplishment or warrior-like victory.

I'm going to London. But it isn't in the way I ever imagined it would be.

36

LARA

"I just put him down for his nap. Poor bugger, he was so tired he could barely keep his eyes open through changing his nappy."

I chuckle to myself as I pad over to Vance, wrapping my arms around him. He's been with us for almost a week since Mason's accident, and I'm falling into the routine I love so much again.

"Come sit with me. I have something to talk to you about." My gorgeous man walks me backward, his hands never leaving my hips.

My heart thuds in my chest wondering what he could want to talk about. He's been telling me for months that he loves me, and I'm a woman who's had a man get down on one knee for her before. Could this be … ?

Last night, I nearly blurted out the words he's been waiting to hear. I was riding Vance, my hair wrapped in his fist and my nails digging into his chest, and he looked up at me like I ruled the entire world, like he'd create a new religion just to worship me.

I have probably always been in love with him, but the love I feel now is just *more*. It's bigger, it has that sense of largeness in your chest that makes you wonder how the universe could contain a feeling this intense.

"What's going on?" I ask, my throat dry.

I swear, if he asks me to marry him right now ...

Of course, I would say yes. The man I've been in love with half my life, the father of my son, the partner who I look forward to coming home to—I've dreamed of this moment.

Vance looks down and then back up into my eyes. "Remus left for another team, to take another keeper position. Niles Harrington just called. They want me to come to London."

Disappointment floods me worse than a boat that's capsized. Embarrassment washes over my cheeks, because how naïve and ridiculously childish could I be? Of course, Vance doesn't have plans to make me his wife. All he's thinking about is Rogue and becoming their starting keeper. As usual.

"Oh, Vance, that's wonderful! It's what you've been waiting for." I try to infuse as much false cheer into my voice as I can.

How can I be incandescently happy about this when it means he'll be leaving us for longer? His life will become chaotic, and who knows how Mason and I will fit into it.

"Well, sort of. They want me to audition for the spot, and are bringing a few other keepers to see which fits best with the squad."

His expression falls, and someone who isn't familiar with every tic of his wouldn't notice. But I do.

"Wait, so you've been working for how long to impress them, to show them how much you deserve this, and they're not giving you the spot outright? Those wankers!" Now I'm enraged for him.

Vance shrugs. "Maybe it's just one more test I have to go through. But that's what I have to talk to you about. I want you and Mason with me. Would you come to London? Maybe just for a few weeks, and then—"

"Vance, I can't just uproot him for a few weeks to live in a hotel. He has preschool, I have to go to work. We have a home here."

"Come on, Lara, we can find him a preschool there." He's not even listening to me.

"You're not even certain you'll be given the starting position, so what's the rush?"

Those chocolate eyes go black with upset. "That's a great vote of confidence, thanks."

His sarcastic tone only serves to annoy me more. Here, I thought he was about to propose. To ask me a question that would solidify our family. Instead, what he's proposing will pull us further apart, or, if he has his way, have Mason and I trail behind him around the world.

"That's not what I mean, and you know it," I snap.

"You just don't want to come. Admit it." This conversation is digressing into our fundamental argument.

"It's the same problem we had before you broke things off. I don't want this life, Vance. I don't want to be a footballer's wife. I don't want to uproot my child and follow you around the world. He needs stability, and I love my job, if that has any weight in the matter."

"You don't want to be a footballer's wife? *Bloody hell*, Lara, then what are we doing? I wouldn't ask you to give up your home, or your job, but you're asking me to give mine up? Everything I've worked for in the last fifteen years, I'm just supposed to walk away?"

Vance blows, shooting up off the sofa.

"If you loved us enough, *yes*."

"If you loved me enough, you wouldn't ask me to."

We're always going to have this sticking point between us. He wants to live his life for the game, and I want him to live life for me. I want a love that means not having to choose anything over it. And with Vance, I will lose. Every time.

"Just go. You're going to anyway. I don't want to fight with you." Because I'm tired, and because it's useless.

"Bloody hell, Lara, you can't even tell me you love me!"

And there it is. Vance throws the one grenade in his arsenal, the one line he knows will cause our whole world to implode. All the hurt I've tried to untangle, the barbed wire wrapped around my heart, sinks deeper into the flesh of the organ he's dismantling once more.

"Why do you think that is? Last time I said it, you left and never looked back. You went gallivanting off into your posh life and left me, a scared, heartbroken teenager with a baby on the way. The last time I told you I loved you, my heart was shattered into a million pieces. Is it any wonder I'm unable to say it now? Look what you're doing; you're about to leave for London with no real timeline of when you'll be back."

Vance's eyes plead with me, but his mouth is a permanent, displeased, straight line. "I would never hurt you like that again. I thought you had more faith in me, in what we've built, than to think that."

But I'm on a role. "Will we ever be enough for you? Will I ever be enough for you? This goddamn football club has stolen the best years of your life, they're wasting your talent, and still, you're going to go kiss their feet and audition for a job that should already be yours."

"You don't understand. You've never understood." His voice is quiet and small.

"I guess I don't." I can taste the heartbreak in my mouth. "But you're going to choose them. You'll go to London because that's where your loyalty lies. So just go."

I can't watch as he walks out the door.

37

VANCE

My knee skids across the pitch, the burn of grass against skin sure to leave a mark.

I barely feel it, though.

I've been at this for hours, footballs flying at every part of my body as I dart from side to side in the net, attempting to block them from going in. My abs and stomach have been beaten in, and I'm sure I'll have bruises all over my ribs when I sink into an ice bath after this. There is a jagged pitch burn running from the middle of my left thigh down past the knee, and I can feel droplets of blood on my sock.

But I can't stop. Around me, the other players of the Rogue Football Club practice drills, passing to each other and cutting back and forth in sprints across the grass. The stadium above us is empty, a silent cathedral that will fill with parishioners in the coming days.

"All right, Morley, you're done. Next!" The trainer who's been firing shots at my body for the last twenty minutes shouts at me to get out of the net.

This is bloody *bullshit*. Having to share time in the net with this German bloke and another keeper from a second tier Italian league. I've done everything Rogue and Niles and the trainers and headmasters have ever asked. I've given up my life, my childhood, time with my parents, and my little family—everything for the good of the club.

I'm clearly the front runner, the most skilled and dedicated keeper on this pitch. And yet, it's been weeks of interviewing and auditioning and proving myself for this position.

The one Lara said should already be mine outright.

God, do I miss her. I miss *them*. It's been weeks since I've seen Mason's face and talking to him for the couple of minutes before Lara takes the phone and says he needs to go to bed is not cutting it. My heart is decimated, and it's my own fault. I know that.

But, she just never understood. She told me to go, to leave. Told me she didn't want to live the life of a footballer's wife which was what she would be no matter if I played at Rogue or not. It's the issue we've been skirting since I vowed to get her back.

This is my life, the sport I love, and if she can't live with that, I'm not sure how we can live *together*. Every morning I wake; my head and heart war with each other.

Push harder on the pitch, you're almost there.

They need you. You love them. Crawl back apologizing.

And each day, I push past it, ignoring all the instincts shouting at me. I'm becoming numb.

Walking to the sidelines, I grab a Gatorade bottle and shoot the sweet ice blue drink into my mouth.

"Looking good in the net, mate. Real good. You're a beast, as usual." Jude comes up, grabbing his own bottle and gulping half of it down.

"Thanks," I respond.

Jude bends down to tighten the laces of his boots and then

stands straight. "You all right? I know your first couple of weeks here can be intense."

"Just fucking tired, mate." I shake my head, not wanting to get into it.

If it looks like I'm reluctant or doubting this process at all, I know Niles may not choose me for the starting job.

"It will all be worth it in the end," Jude tells me solemnly.

That's the thing though ... "Will it?"

Kingston drops into step with us. "It might. It might not."

"Thanks for eavesdropping, arse." Jude glares at him. "Don't listen to him. It will be. This is the dream, remember?"

For the longest time, it was the dream. And then I met my son.

"It took me getting demoted to Nartanica to realize that football isn't everything. It's the sport I bloody love, yes, but it isn't life and death." Kingston shrugs, being insightful and genuine for once in his prankster life.

Last year, our mate got into a lot of trouble both on and off the pitch, and Niles loaned him out to a fourth-tier team in the middle of nowhere. It forced him to grow up, to realize what was important, and I think he's better off because of it.

And now, his words sink in hard. "If Poppy asked you to give it up, would you?"

Kingston regards me, and I hear Jude inhale sharply. "Why? Are you think about doing that for Lara?"

"Aria wouldn't ask that of me. She knows what football means to me." Jude throws his two cents in.

My head snaps to him. "I wasn't asking you."

While I love Jude like a brother, his opinion in this situation is biased and skewed. Football, to him, is life. He lost his parents as a child, and this sport has given him the opportunity to survive. Jude is this country's next bloody savior, the hype around him is insane. Plus, he and Aria are not Lara and me.

"I don't know that she would ask. But, if she did ... yes. I probably would. This sport is so finite, it's fickle and tosses us away like rubbish after it's done with us. Poppy is my forever. She's the one I have to answer to at the end of the day, and if you don't believe you have to answer to your woman, well, mate, I don't know what to tell you."

My friend smirks and his joking nature makes me feel marginally better.

What if I don't get this starting job? Would Lara take me back, even if she wasn't my first choice? I doubted this.

And I've already royally cocked us up once and vowed to her that I'd fight through hell to get her and Mason back.

But when it really comes down to it, have I? I've done exactly what I did to her the first time. Exactly what I said I wouldn't do.

Looking around the Rogue stadium, the church I've always hoped to worship at, I know I'm about to make the biggest decision of my life.

38

LARA

I'm sitting at the breakfast table, two weeks after Vance left for London, and Mason asks me to put hot sauce on his eggs.

That's when I lose it.

After fetching the hot sauce, and pouring the tiniest drop of it on his eggs, I shut myself in the bathroom and sob. Because my son is only asking for it to imitate how his father eats his own eggs.

I kept it together for a while there, after he left. I had to, or at least I told myself I did, for Mason. For as long as I can remember, I've muscled through my heartbreak and feelings for my son, for the good of our life, and so I went into autopilot. Our routine fell back into the half-conscious state it operated in before Vance came back and promised he'd make me fall in love with him again.

It's far too late for that. I've been in love with him since I saw him that first day across the street in our childhood neighborhood. But now it's even worse. Leave me once, shame on you. Leave me twice, shame on me.

I should have known it would end. What I didn't expect,

when I was sobbing in the bathroom while Mason ate his eggs with hot sauce, was to feel as much guilt as I did.

I've asked him to sacrifice. Every time, it's been me telling him he needs to prove his love by giving up something he holds dear. When we were together, I wanted him to myself. I wanted to be more important than football.

When I chose not to tell him about Mason, I held it against him that he didn't know his son. And when he wanted to try, I pushed him away. When the media attacked us, Vance was the one who took the brunt of the hit and decided to say nothing.

It's taken me this long to realize that not everything ends in loneliness. We're not my parents. Times can be tough, and love can still remain. It's what's in the bones, the foundation, of a relationship that determines if it has staying power.

Like a lightbulb flicking on in my head, I stand up off the bathroom floor. He's sacrificed for us as much as he could. Now, it's time to sacrifice for him.

So, I called my mother, packed bags for both Mason and I, dropped him off, and steered my old, beat-up car toward London.

I've never driven into the city before, and not only am I on the edge of an anxiety attack due to the fact that I'm about to beg for Vance's forgiveness and admit my undying love, but blimey, I've almost gotten murdered by a taxi twice.

When I finally find a parking spot in a garage three streets over from where Vance is staying in temporary player housing, my hands are shaking. I've been thinking about what I'll say the entire ride here, and now that I'm about to ring up to his flat, I can't remember a thing I rehearsed.

All I know is that I've been so, so wrong. I've wanted so much to cling to my independence, to my need not to be tamed. The grit in my bones that wouldn't allow me to heed control to anyone, especially a man. I didn't want to end up in a marriage, and subsequent divorce, like my parents. And with a love as intense and massive as the one between Vance and I, a chemistry like that can go volatile quickly.

Blimey, I've been so selfish. I've been a twit. Look at what's right in front of me. A man who has tried diligently to prove to me that he's going to love me, and his son, for the rest of his life.

I'm going to promise him the same thing.

Pressing the button, I wait for him to pick up.

A few seconds later, his gruff, deep voice comes through the small intercom.

"Hello?"

I clear my throat. "Vance? It's me. Can I come up?"

A beat passes. "Lara?"

"Yes," I answer timidly.

I wouldn't be surprised if he didn't want to see me. I've been acting like a spoiled brat since he left for London, not even allowing him to address me on the phone calls he made to speak to Mason.

The buzzer for the door sounds, and I wrench it open, squeezing through before Vance can come down and throw me out.

I take the lift to the fifth floor, the one I know Vance is on due to the intercom at the front of the building. When I step out onto the floor and peer down the hall, there he is.

It's been weeks since I've held him in my gaze, and instantly, butterflies flutter in my stomach. Vance's appearance is always shocking; the sheer size of him dwarfs any space he occupies. He's impossibly tall, stupendously brawny and to those who don't know his soft-spoken soul, intimidating. His inky brown eyes search mine, and I want so terribly to just run into his arms and break down into a sappy mess.

But I owe this to him, to admit to my feelings the way he's admitted to his.

"How did you ..."

He seems stunned that I'm even standing in this hallway, and I walk to him until we're almost toe to toe.

"I had a whole speech I thought up in the car." My voice is nervous, and I smile a little because I'm jumping out of my skin. "But now that I'm standing here, I can't remember anything I wanted to say."

"You ... I thought we were through. You told me to go," he says.

A deep breath works its way through my lungs. This is it.

"I'm terrified, Vance. I'm scared you'll walk out on me again. Only this time, it's not just me. Mason ... that would destroy him. I want you to accomplish everything you've worked for, but I'm so bloody scared this will all end the way it did last time. And I'm hopelessly in love with you. Maybe even more than I was when I was sixteen. Because now, I've seen you as a father. I've watched you tuck our son in, and I've made a home with you. I'm shaking in my boots thinking I'll lose that. But none of the fear would be worth it if I just ran scared. So, here we are. I love you. I'm saying it, out loud. I love you. Wherever you are, that's where I want to be. That's where our son should be."

Well, that was pretty ace. Not the speech I rehearsed, but muscle memory did its job brilliantly I'd say.

"It doesn't matter," he says, a final-like note in his voice.

My heart shatters, and I'm so crushed my voice comes out like a broken thing. "Why?"

"Because I signed with the Brighton Football Club about two hours ago."

I blink, and everything slams into me at once. My heart into my ribs. Reality into my brain. Tears to my ducts. And the clear-cut fact that Vance chose me at the exact moment I chose him.

"You what?"

Vance motions to the bags behind him, the ones I hadn't noticed until now sitting in the doorway of the flat.

"I've been on the phone with the Brighton manager for the last week, on and off. I told Niles I wouldn't audition for the position anymore. Didn't even stay to hear if he'd name me the starter out of pressure or threat, because I don't care anymore. Rogue has never repaid the loyalty and respect I've shown them, so I'm looking out for me. I'm looking out for us. Playing for Brighton gives me everything I want. I don't want to sacrifice anymore."

He picked us. Even after I pushed him away for the umpteenth time, he still chose us. Just like he promised he would.

"Can you tell me again?" Vance's voice is so serious, but he still hasn't touched me yet.

"Tell you ... oh." A smile stretches my cheeks. "I love you, Vance Morley. Against reason, and my independent soul, and even though you talk about football constantly, I love you."

Vance closes his eyes, and a small grin works its way over his lips. "Been waiting a long time to hear that."

And now he reaches for me. In the middle of the hallway to a flat he was just about to leave, the man I've been in love with for as long as I can remember plants a scorching, branding kiss on my lips.

He is mine, and I am his, all of our bruises and thorns accounted for.

In the end, we sacrificed for each other.

39

VANCE

A wave crashes onto the shore, spraying tiny specks of foam at me that dot my cheeks and wet my hair.

The air is still crisp and frigid, the scent of salt stinging my nostrils but also waking my system up in a way that nothing else ever can.

Now that I've made the decision, my soul feels more settled than it ever has in my short twenty-two years. The fact that my choice was my hometown, returning to the place that I feel most complete, well, that's just the cherry on top.

"Daddy, watch!" Mason chirps.

He picks up a stone, the same stones his mother sat on the first time I kissed her, and throws it into the ocean.

Lara and I have been trying to teach him to skip it, which is difficult in waves this choppy, but he gets such a kick out of it that I can't help but bend to his request to come out to the beach. Plus, now that I get to spend almost every day with him, it's hard to say no when all my boy wants to do is explore and play.

"Nice one, bud! Two skips that time." I hold up my hand for a high five, and his tiny hand slaps my palm.

"Again!" Mason shouts. *Everything* is again.

I've been in Brighton for a month, and since the day I walked out of the Rogue stadium, essentially giving up the starting keeper job in favor of being sold to my hometown club, I've never regretted it.

Sometimes, dreams change. For as long as I can remember, I've wanted to be the starting keeper for Rogue Football Club. I bled myself dry, pushed myself harder than everyone else, only for it to not work out. Or maybe it would have.

That's the thing. By the time I got close to it, that was no longer my dream. Now my dream is to be as close as possible to the woman I love and our son. My dream is to wake up next to Lara in the morning, to watch Mason learn how to play football or rugby or do theater or whatever it is that his dream is.

Dreams can be selfish, but they can also be about showing up for the ones you love as much as you can.

Taking the starting keeper position at Brighton gives me that option. I get to play in the top football league in England, but I also get to spend every night with my family. I get to raise my son and flirt with the woman I plan to make my wife. Very soon, if I have a say in it.

Brighton gave me a solid contract, one that will set Lara and me up for a very long time to come. My teammates are ace, and the manager and trainers are trustworthy and fair. Playing for them has been a welcome change.

The only twinge of sorrow comes when I think about Jude and Kingston playing on a team that doesn't feature me. We worked for a long time to be able to play together, the three horsemen of the football apocalypse. But in the end, they're happy for me. And I get to talk shite to them when they try to score on me whenever Brighton plays Rogue.

"All right, you two, time for lunch. I need a good cup of tea to warm my bones up." Lara wraps her arms around herself, even though she's bundled in a thick coat and mittens.

She looks absolutely scrumptious. When Mason goes down for his nap, I'm going to convince her to "nap" with me, too.

"What Mummy says, goes." I raise an eyebrow at my son, acting as if I would let him stay out here longer but she's the final word.

"Chocolate biscuit?" Mason allows me to pick him up without protesting, but only because he knows I'll say yes to a pre-nap snack.

"Of course." I nod, wanting one for myself, too.

Lara rolls her eyes. "You're going to rot his teeth."

With our son resting on one hip, I wrap my other arm around her shoulders as we walk up the beach. "Eh, let him have a little fun."

Our feet tread over the same stones that Lara and I grew up running on. Here, we became the people we are today. This is the place where I first admitted how I always adored her from afar. It's where we first truly *saw* each other, down to a soul deep level.

David Grey's voice plays in my head, the same song that played on the beach all those Christmases ago.

Because this year's love ... it's going to last.

40

LARA

"Fine. I guess I can see why you like it here."

Kingston grumbles into his omelet, cutting off a huge bite and scarfing it down.

Aria chuckles. "Oh, Kingy, don't act like you didn't love the boat ride we took last time. He's talked about it every time I've seen him since."

"And he even mentioned looking at property down here. A holiday home, I believe he called it." Poppy rolls her eyes.

The group of us, sitting around the table at our favorite local breakfast spot, all laugh.

It's the gang's third visit to us in the last couple of months, because I'm not sure that Vance, Jude, and Kingston can operate if they don't see each other every few weeks. Not that I mind, I enjoy getting together with all of them. Poppy and Aria have become close confidants, especially because they know first-hand what it's like as the other half of a relationship with an athlete. When I feel like I can't make it through one more day without Vance, if he's traveling internationally for a match, I call either one of them and they sympathize, talk me down, and then gossip about any errant thing to get my mind off of it.

"Do it, mate. We'd love to have you ocean-side." Vance nods as he cuts up pieces of pancake for Mason, who is sitting in his high chair coloring.

Is it ridiculous that just watching him cut up food for our toddler makes me want to shag him?

"Nah, mate, I couldn't give up London. She's my mistress. But nowhere near as fit as you, love." Kingston cups Poppy's chin and kisses her.

Aria chuckles. "I could never imagine Kingston living anywhere else *besides* London. Me on the other hand? I'm beginning to love New York."

Jude gives his fiancée a sliding glance. "Don't get any big ideas. I'm too damn good to play in that thing the Americans consider a proper football league."

Aria recently kicked off a tour that will take her to cities around the world for the next six months. She and Jude haven't done any wedding planning thus far, though I think it'll be a small, but swanky, affair. Neither has much family, and aside from the people sitting at this table, there aren't many other people they'll invite.

"I'm only teasing you, love. I wouldn't dare take the prince of the pitch away from his adoring fans." She steals a piece of bacon off of Jude's plate.

"You would not believe how many of my students ask if I can get your autograph for them," I tell Jude.

Or how many ask what Vance thinks about that weekend's match. They're all still flabbergasted that I'm with the keeper of the hometown football club.

"I could do them one better and come in for a lesson," he offers.

While the students would be completely chuffed with me, I have to decline. "The only football legend I bring into my classroom is my husband. Brighton pride, loves."

Vance winks at me, while Jude and Kingston roll their eyes and huff. "I've been into her classroom. The kids love me. But I'm pretty sure they love her more."

He's right, mostly. After a rather bumpy start to the year, the students I have in my classes have turned out to be pretty great. They've opened up, taken my guidance, and even read most of the books I've assigned.

School is almost out, and I'm looking to the time off in the summer. Typically, I've worked in the past, either as a tutor or at a local nursery school. But with Vance's salary, I won't have to do that anymore. Three glorious months of almost every day with Mason? I'm so excited I could scream.

Plus, it just so happens that the premier league season finish lines up with when I'm done with school. He's been brilliant this season for Brighton, becoming one of the leaders at the club and helping to win matches. The club is set to finish fifth in the standings, three places higher than they did last year.

Vance will be off from May to August, though not playing matches doesn't mean he won't have to go to work every day. Training, some friendly matches, and national team practices will take place. At least he gets to play with Jude and Kingston on the national team.

As if reading my mind, Jude pipes up, "Bloody pumped to workout in London with you, mate."

"Me too, can't wait to get out onto that pitch. Two more years and we'll be hoisting that World Cup trophy." Vance's brown eyes sparkle with excitement.

"You bet your arse we will." Kingston shovels more food into his mouth.

He'll be back and forth to London through the summer as the national team trains together. But luckily, we'll be able to go with him. I'm thrilled myself to be able to explore the city and to adventure with Mason.

It doesn't escape my mind that we'll never have to worry about money again. I struggled quite a lot in the beginning, having a baby at the age of twenty. Even before that, when I was growing up, I never had much. Obviously, I'm not with Vance for his money, remember I hid the existence of his son? Although the papers love to call me a gold digger. Anyhow, it brings an odd sense of relief knowing I won't have to hustle every minute of my life to survive, much less try to provide a better life for my son.

Vance didn't even ask if I want to leave my job, he knew what the answer would be. I love what I do, and I'm not the type of woman who could stay home. I told him from the start, I wouldn't be a footballer's wife. And now I am, but I'm still my own person.

He's promised to take me to Greece at some point during the summer. I'm just looking forward to a repeat experience like our nights on the Canary Islands.

"I literally cannot believe this." Stef, who is sitting on my right, blinks again, pretty much like she's been doing the entire meal.

She's still in shock over the fact that these are my people now. I guess it's all pretty strange, who can say that they're closest friends are some of the greatest athletes, renowned singer, and model in England? I never thought I'd be able to say that. My work mate, and overall confidant, is still a constant in our lives. Stef comes over for dinner most weeks, stays with me when Vance travels, and keeps me entertained enough at work so I don't go mental on my students.

I clap her on the shoulder. "Most days, I can't either."

Because I can't. There was a point in my life where I thought I'd be in the strife of loving a man who couldn't dedicate himself solely to me forever. There were days, when Mason was first born, that I never thought I could get out from under the massive weight of stress always sitting on my shoulders.

And now, as I sit here at a table full of friends who I care very deeply about and who care very deeply about me, I can't help but look to the man sitting across from me.

Vance Morley. From that night on the beach all those years ago to now, how much have we been through? I knew, from the moment he stepped into my space on those rocks, with the waves drowning out all sound and the black night almost blinding us, that I wouldn't be able to see anything else when he was in my sights.

If it's even possible, I fall more in love with him each day. There are layers to our relationship now, ones where I love him because of how he makes me feel, but also unspoken things like how brilliant of a father he is.

"Ugh." Poppy interrupts my thoughts, slouching against the booth as her face turns a pale shade of green.

"You okay?" Kingston turns to her immediately, pressing the back of his hand against her forehead.

"Just, you know ..." She smiles sheepishly at him.

Holy bollocks.

"You okay, Poppy?" Vance asks, looking concerned.

Kingston looks at his fiancée, who is set to be his wife in just four short months. "She's fine, just has a bit of morning sickness."

"Oh my God! What!" Aria almost jumps out of the booth.

"Mate! Congratulations!" Jude does that thing with Kingston that blokes do when trying to manly hug each other.

I had a feeling, recently, when Poppy mentioned something about not wanting to have a glass of wine, but I wasn't sure. And then she turned green just now, and I knew it before Kingston even confirmed.

"Happy for you, mate. It will be the best role of your life."

Vance nods sagely at his friend, because they're going to be in the same club now.

Poppy reaches a hand out to me. "I wanted to complain to you so many times, but didn't want to jinx it."

"I completely understand, and I'm so happy for you. You're going to be the best mother. And I have ginger candies that will get you through that morning sickness." I squeeze her hand, smiling as wide as my cheeks will let me.

She's about to go on the most frustrating, most tiring, most incredible journey of her life. Poppy and Kingston will be wonderful parents, mostly because they love each other so much. From their tragic pasts, they'll create a home full of support and adoration.

Just like Vance and I have. Out of all the heartbreak, struggle, and pain, we've created a family that cannot be broken apart. Forged in steel and sealed with the promise of our love, there is nothing we can't face together now.

Vance is the anchor that centers us. He's our steadying presence, the reliable, dependable force that will never let us down. As long as I live, I'll vow to be the ocean that tries to stir him up. It's our dynamic, how we work well together.

For as different as we are, there is no one on earth I'd rather swim through life with. And isn't that what it's all about?

EPILOGUE
VANCE

Three Years Later

Pushing through the door, my heart races frantically, waiting to capture a glimpse of her.

They made me leave, those bastards. I almost socked a nurse in the jaw, that's how fierce my protective instincts are right now. And if I don't hold Lara in my sight soon, I'm going to turn into the rage-filled animal everyone assumes I am.

What is it that they say about the quiet ones?

"I'm right here, love."

Her voice, now much calmer than it was when I left the room.

Lara.

My eyes lock onto her, lying there in that stark white hospital bed. When I left her, those denim blue eyes were twisted in agony, and I couldn't do anything to help.

Now, she's serene. A bloody angel resting back on the pillows, her blond hair floating around her head like a halo. She's gorgeous, and although I can't see the movements, I know the bump swelling the sheets over her belly is rippling with movement.

Our baby girl is on her way.

"How are you feeling?" I rush to her side, gripping her small hand in my big one, careful not to squeeze with too much pressure.

"I'm fine. Better. So much better. Anyone who tells you not to get the drugs is a bloody sadist." My wife chuckles.

I smooth my finger over the diamond band around her ring finger, the place I put it almost two and a half years ago. Once I decided to sign with Brighton, I packed my things from the academy and immediately went home to Lara and Mason. About a month after that, we moved into our charming house right on the beach; Lara wanted something completely opposite of my parent's home and I gave her whatever she wanted. Hell, I've been giving her whatever she wants since the day she took London by storm and told me she loved me back.

"I hate seeing you in pain," I lament, kissing her forehead and brushing back strands of her cornsilk hair.

"Then you must have really hated the last nine months," she jokes.

"The exact opposite, actually. I'm going to miss this." My hand skims over her bump.

"I'm having labor contractions and you're getting randy about my massive stomach. Men." She rolls her eyes.

Watching her body grow pregnant with our daughter has been incredible. There is nothing like sharing this experience with the woman you love, and it has made me happier than I've ever been. Being able to see Mason so excited about becoming a big brother comes in as a close second.

Our son started primary school last week and is home with my parents. They're all waiting with not so well-handled anxious energy, as they text me every other minute to ask if the baby has made her arrival.

Lara's water broke about seven hours ago, and she muscled through the pain as long as she could before it got so intense she was begging for the epidural. I've been by her side the entire time, and we're so close to meeting our girl that I know I have to be her anchor right now. The mighty force that will ground her through the hardest of waves.

"All right, love, it's time to push. The doctor said it's time." I kiss her cheeks, wishing I could take the brunt of the pain.

"I'm scared." Now Lara's face transforms into a mask of fear, which is something I rarely see from my warrior of a wife.

"There is no need to be. I'm right here. Just think about holding our daughter in your arms, and scream as loud as you want," I tell her.

It takes almost forty minutes, but in an instant, I hear a cry and our daughter comes into the world. Lara is crying, and one of the nurses bundles the baby up in a blanket and then hands her to my wife. I watch in amazement as the suckling newborn presses her check to her mum's chest, and instantly calms.

The baby has a full head of black hair, and I run a hand over it as tears fill my eyes.

"She is so beautiful." I breathe.

"Another baby who looks just like you." Lara grins a watery smile. "Will there ever be one who resembles me?"

"We'll just have to keep trying." I smirk at her.

If she'll let me, I'll have an entire football team with her.

We cuddle the baby for what feels like forever before the doctors and nurses come in to run some routine tests.

After that, Lara and the baby sleep for a while, both of them rightfully exhausted from creating a life and coming into the world respectively. I just stare, astonished at the miracle that is my life. How do I deserve these people to love me, this family to take care of?

My wife is just starting to flutter her eyes open when Mason rushes in, a bouquet of flowers in one hand and a plush pink bunny in the other.

"Daddy! Mummy! I have a sister!" His little five-year-old body is humming with elation.

"Yes you do, love." Lara receives him, kissing and side hugging him from where he stands on the floor. "Come on up, get comfy, and you can hold her."

I go to her bassinet while Lara gets Mason ready and demonstrates how to hold her. The baby curls up into me when I pick her up, and I'm scared I might break her. Something this precious, this delicate, and she's put her trust in me to take care of her? Blimey, I'm one lucky bastard.

Watching Mason hold his baby sister is one of my top five favorite moments I've ever lived through. She sneezes at one point, and he giggles as if it's the funniest thing in the world.

My parents come in next, cooing over the baby, and Lara's Mum isn't far behind. Stef stops in for a visit, and then the cavalry arrives.

Poppy, Kingston, Jude, and Aria all file into the room, with presents and smiles galore.

None of them are rookies at the labor and delivery wing at this point. Poppy and King have Julia, their two-year-old daughter, and a little boy due any day now. The girls like to joke that our daughter has a future boyfriend. I told Kingston I'll have his boy's bollocks if he touches my daughter.

Jude and Aria have three-month-old twin boys, Benjamin and Brenton, and are currently in sleep deprivation hell. But, they both refuse to use the luxury of nannies, which they could certainly afford. Secretly, I think they're attempting to become vampires in order to stay up and stare at their babies all hours of the day. That's how much they love being parents.

They take turns passing the baby around, all melting at the sight of her.

"And do you have a name?" Aria cradles our daughter, smiling down at her and then back up to us.

Lara and I look at each other, and she tells them. "Dorian. Dorian Roberta Morley."

We picked her name out months ago, when Lara was looking through a baby book. In Greek, Dorian means "of the sea," and if that isn't just perfect. The love between her mother and father was born of the sea, so it fit.

And while we were picking the baby's name, we also decided to legally change Mason's surname. He'd been born a Logan, but as he is half mine, and our family is a unit now, Lara and I wanted all of us to be a part of our clan.

"Beautiful. Just beautiful." Poppy nods, rubbing her belly. "This boy can't wait to meet Dorian."

I glare at Kingston. "I'll kick his arse, I swear."

"No shite talking when the little bloke isn't even hearthside yet. All right, we'll get out of your hair. See you on the pitch in a week, mate. We're going to kick your arse."

Rogue is playing Brighton next week, and it will be my first match back after the short paternity leave I'm taking. I don't need to argue with him, I'll shut him and Jude out of the goal so hard, they'll see clean sheets in their nightmares.

Once they're gone, everyone naps again, knackered from all the love and guests. But me? I walk to Dorian's bassinet and scoop her up, going to sit in the rocking chair in our hospital room.

Of all the things I've envisioned for my life, this is the furthest thing from what I dreamed.

That's the thing about the universe, though, it laughs at the plans you make. Because it already has plans for you.

These people, my amazing wife, brilliant son, and beautiful newborn daughter, they are the dreams I never knew I had. The ones that have eclipsed everything else.

Of all the grouchy, silent blokes in the world, I'm the luckiest. And I've been through enough to know that I'll never take that for granted.

Ready for another sports romance series? Dive into *Warning Track* and meet the Callahans, a small town family baseball dynasty.

Read the rest of The Rogue Academy series, available now!

The Second Coming
The Lion Heart
The Mighty Anchor

ALSO BY CARRIE AARONS

Do you want your **FREE** Carrie Aarons eBook?

All you have to do is **sign up for my newsletter**, and you'll immediately receive your free book!

Then, check out all of my books, available in Kindle Unlimited!

Standalones:

If Only in My Dreams

Foes & Cons

Love at First Fight

Nerdy Little Secret

That's the Way I Loved You

Fool Me Twice

Hometown Heartless

The Tenth Girl

You're the One I Don't Want

Privileged

Elite

Red Card

Down We'll Come, Baby

As Long As You Hate Me

On Thin Ice

All the Frogs in Manhattan

Save the Date

Melt

When Stars Burn Out

Ghost in His Eyes

Kissed by Reality

The Prospect Street Series:

Then You Saw Me

The Callahan Family Series:

Warning Track

Stealing Home

Check Swing

Control Artist

Tagging Up

The Rogue Academy Series:

The Second Coming

The Lion Heart

The Mighty Anchor

The Nash Brothers Series:

Fleeting

Forgiven

Flutter

Falter

The Flipped Series:

Blind Landing

Grasping Air

The Captive Heart Duet:

Lost

Found

The Over the Fence Series:

Pitching to Win

Hitting to Win

Catching to Win

Box Sets:

The Nash Brothers Box Set

The Complete Captive Heart Duet

The Over the Fence Box Set

ABOUT THE AUTHOR

Author of romance novels such as Fool Me Twice and Love at First Fight, Carrie Aarons writes books that are just as swoon-worthy as they are sarcastic. A former journalist, she prefers the love stories of her imagination, and the athleisure dress code, much better.

When she isn't writing, Carrie is busy binging reality TV, having a love/hate relationship with cardio, and trying not to burn dinner. She lives in the suburbs of New Jersey with her husband, two children and ninety-pound rescue pup.

Please join her readers group, Carrie's Charmers, to get the latest on new books, exclusive excerpts and fun giveaways.

You can also find Carrie at these places:
Website
Amazon
Facebook
Instagram
TikTok
Goodreads

Made in the USA
Middletown, DE
29 October 2021